BEYOND REVENGE

Mischievous Malamute Mystery Series Book 2

HARLEY CHRISTENSEN

For Naoisha

CHAPTER ONE

Mr. Sandman was mocking me. If the night sweats and nightmares hadn't been the proof I needed, whacking my head on the nightstand after a particularly restless episode should have clued me in. I rubbed the knot that formed, convinced it was an exercise devilishly crafted to test my patience and likely, my sanity. Grumpy, I mentally added "Minion of Hell" to the sandman's epitaph as I struggled to untangle myself from the remnants of a tortured slumber.

Finally free from the destruction that had once resembled a bed, I plopped my feet on the floor. The coolness nipped at my toes as I glanced back at my bedmate, who managed to snore contently after successfully stealing the better part of the blankets. His tongue wiggled rhythmically as he exhaled, a sign he was having good doggie dreams. I really had to stop sharing my bed with a ninety-eight pound Alaskan Malamute.

Tomorrow, I sighed.

I padded down the hall, drawn toward the light emanating from the kitchen, which usually meant Leah was still up working on an assignment. After our last adventure, Leah Campbell, my best friend and now roommate, had thrown in the towel at her newspaper gig for a life of freelance writing and researching. She had no trouble drumming up work, but felt the transition necessitated a change in address.

I peered into the kitchen. My hunch was right, Leah *had* been up working on an assignment—as verified by the mass of paper strewn across every available surface—but apparently, at some point her brain had given in to other ideas. Leah was now sprawled face down—in all her drooling glory—on top of the kitchen island. I was pretty sure there was a stove under there somewhere. *Comfy?* I thought to myself. Every few seconds, she muttered something that sounded eerily like "brownies," though it could have been "bunnies." Regardless, she was obviously stressed about the project at hand.

I removed a spiral binder from beneath her head, hoping she'd thank me for it later, despite the enchanting imprint it left on her check. She was lucky I didn't have my camera handy. Nah, I wouldn't do that to her, though it was fun to jangle her chain every once in a while.

"Yoohoo, Sleeping Beauty, your prince has arrived and is about to storm the castle to avenge your honor. Lest he see his betrothed drooling or he might choose to run off with the witty best friend."

"Shut it…off…" was the muttered response, followed by a colorful variation of "go away."

"Perhaps he'll be so overcome with appreciation of my stunning features, we'll end up running off to Vegas to meet Elvis at The Little White Chapel?"

"Don't care…sleeping here…"

"Ok then, an early morning smooch from Nicoh?"

"That beast so much as breathes in my direction, I'll withhold snacks, indefinitely," Leah mumbled as she opened one eye to glare at me. "Seriously? Can't a girl take a nap around this place without being harassed, or threatened with doggie breath?"

"Tough assignment?" I asked as I began collecting the hand-written notes that had fallen to the floor.

"Tough assignment, tough night," she replied. "Have been doing research all night for the Dynamic Duo."

I nodded. Several of her freelance projects had been contracted by Abe and Elijah Stanton, two brothers who ran a private investigations firm in Los Angeles. We had met them through their involvement with my sister's case a few months earlier. After Leah left the newspaper, they had hired her to research a few of their other cases. Currently, she was embroiled in the details surrounding a seven-year-old missing person's case.

"Starting to look like this gal purposely left a bad situation. Hard to make her reappear when she's worked so hard to escape in the first place." A hint of sadness filled her voice as she yawned.

"What will you do?"

Leah shrugged. "I was hired to do research, which I did. The rest is up to Abe and Elijah."

I handed her the notes I had collected and squeezed her arm. "It's all you can do, Leah. It's in their hands now. You know they'll do the right thing."

She nodded, absently pulling on the short tufts of blond hair that framed her face. While her eyes were puffy and the binder imprint still graced her cheek, I marveled at how she managed to look so good at this time of day. It was her quick wit and smart mouth that usually got her into trouble, though I had a sneaking suspicion she'd caught the attention of the older Stanton brother, Abe, whether she realized it or not. Leah yawned again while glancing at the clock, and after noting the early hour, frowned as she looked at me squarely.

"Still having the dreams," she commented. I nodded, though it hadn't been a question. Leah bowed her head in a quick acknowledgment.

"You ready for tonight?" This time I shrugged. Honestly, I wasn't sure.

We had been recruited by Charlie Wilson, an old high school friend, to help with the condominium-warming party he was throwing at his penthouse that evening. I was using the term "friend" a bit freely, as neither Leah nor I were in Charlie's social circle. We were more or less unpaid help, performing menial tasks, though Charlie insisted it was our particular talents he was interested in procuring for the party.

Charlie was also a frequent client of my photography services, a business I'd aptly named Mischievous Malamute after a few innocent episodes involving Nicoh during some of my earlier assignments. Misbehaved companion aside, Charlie had recruited me for my photographer's eye—as he'd phrased it—requesting my presence during setup to ensure the party's look and feel met with his exacting standards.

He claimed he wanted Leah on hand at the party for her contacts at the paper and within the community, with the hope she could nudge details of the festivities into the appropriate society pages, and into the right ears.

In reality, Charlie needed our help because he was short-handed after firing his personal assistant. Now persona non grata, Arch Underwood had reportedly been booted from the penthouse after having the audacity to don attire that clashed with his surroundings and apparently, Charlie's sensibility. From my experience Charlie favored steel, black or white—meaning any splash of color, or anything denim, not only offended him, it got his blood percolating. Therefore, for his crimes against all things monochromatic, Arch was promptly ejected, leaving Charlie without his minion.

I wasn't Arch's replacement—I did have my own business with my own clients, after all—but every time I was around Charlie, people managed to assume I was his new Girl Friday. I was convinced Charlie had something to do with that, the irony being I wasn't exactly color-coded to his standards, either. Why I was elected to help him with his party was beyond me.

In case you were wondering, my name is Arianna Jackson. My friends call me AJ, or Ajax if I'm being particularly precocious. I'm a twenty-something freelance photographer who, as I briefly mentioned, lives with my ex-reporter best female friend, Leah. Of course, there's also my best canine friend, Nicoh, who possesses marginal manners and an extreme attitude—the dog, not the girl. We reside in the desert setting of Phoenix, Arizona in a home that belonged to my parents before their deaths in a plane crash a few years prior. Until recently, we believed the crash had been a tragic accident. That was until I found my twin sister—a sibling I hadn't previously known existed—violently murdered. My life had changed forever in that moment, replaced by a series of long-buried secrets—the kind of secrets only the dead could reveal. Well, the dead and a couple of murderous wackadoos, as it turned out.

Long story short, both our adoptive parents had been murdered, along with several other innocent people. All because of a very deadly secret that started with our biological parents, who had been the first to perish trying to protect it. As it turned out, Victoria and I were that secret. When Victoria put the pieces together and tried to warn me, she was rewarded with death. Now I'm the sole protector of the secret—the one who holds the key. Literally.

I know I should take solace in the fact the murderers were apprehended and incarcerated, but I don't. I can't. My very existence poses a threat. So while I try to live my life in spite of this challenge, it manages to creep into my thoughts on occasion and more frequently, into my dreams. Fortunately, my days are filled with enough distractions to prevent me from obsessing over them —the most recent of which happens to be named Charlie.

I shook my head in the negative to Leah's question—no one would ever be prepared for one of his shindigs, or for Charlie.

I would soon come to fully appreciate the irony of that.

* * *

Nicoh emerged, suddenly aware he had been missing the action in the kitchen and a possible snacking opportunity, his piercing whoo-whoos notifying us he was awake and in immediate need of attention. Had it not been for his soft brown eyes, almost megaphone-like ears and endearing smile, it would have been annoying. Somehow, I think the little stinker knew this about himself and used it to its full advantage. Like I said, he's a stinker. But I love him. And, considering my not-so-much of a relationship with a certain homicide detective by the name of Ramirez, Nicoh was *the* man in my life. Granted, some people might consider the non-human members of their households—canines, felines, bovines, etc.—to be mere pets, Nicoh was anything but. He was my companion, my confidante and sometimes, even my hero. As a bonus, he never judged me when I ate too many fries, left the house wearing the clothes I'd slept in or failed to brush my teeth. I couldn't very well complain, could I? He was mostly—if I overlooked the late night cover-stealing and occasional doggie-breath —the perfect pal.

And while Leah is pretty darn good, Nicoh is a natural born jerk-o-meter. If Nicoh doesn't like a guy, they tend to scurry away, man-parts covered. Yes, scurry. Perhaps the honker on an Alaskan Malamute should be registered as a lethal weapon. Go on —look it up if you don't believe me. I'll wait.

That being said, Nicoh and his nozzle were presently on the prowl for one thing and one thing alone. Breakfast. It was still early, so Leah and I hadn't eaten yet. Nicoh wasn't convinced and placed his massive head on the counter to investigate. After rooting around in Leah's notes for a few seconds, he sniffed in disgust and proceeded to look for errant crumbs on the kitchen floor.

"Uh, those were my papers that your dog just boogered on," Leah groused, her brow furrowed.

"He did not booger on anything," I huffed in response, though a smirk played at the corner of my mouth.

"You'd think with all that training he's had, he'd have better manners," she retorted, her own smile forming as she swatted Nicoh's curly tail. Nicoh rewarded her by swooping in and licking her from the crown of her tousled head to the bottom of her perky face.

"Ack!" she cried in mock horror, hopping off the counter and running down the hall to her room.

I laughed at her hasty retreat and smiled at Nicoh, who swished his tailed wildly from side to side in delight before whoo-whooing again, a reminder that he had still not received his requisite nourishment. After all, who was I to make the big beast wait?

* * *

An hour later, Nicoh had been properly fed, I had showered and collected the items needed for my trip to Charlie's. Before leaving, I paused to knock on Leah's door, but upon noting the absence of Duran Duran or The Beastie Boys blaring from beneath the threshold, assumed she had decided to sleep in her bed for a change and left her alone. We hopped in my old Mini Cooper and headed to the Tempe Town Lake condominium where Charlie lived and was holding his party.

It was early and traffic was still light, a refreshing change from the usual bumper-to-bumper of rush hour, so we made good time. With Arch no longer in the picture, I figured he'd be short-handed and appreciate my early arrival. As expected, Stuart

Klein, the jovial doorman waved us through. Nicoh and I were frequent visitors, though I suspected Nicoh was his favorite.

Upon exiting the elevator that deposited us into Charlie's penthouse, I stopped short. Arch was back at his post, a small desk Charlie had installed in the entryway just outside the elevator. His gaze was steely as we stepped into his territory, lips curled in distaste. Despite his cool appraisal, I found myself stifling a chuckle. As usual, his facial expressions managed to look as though someone had spiked his latte with vinegar.

He was, however, always fastidiously dressed and today was no exception, though his current ensemble was more toned-down than usual and consisted of a gray silk shirt, matching tie and black slacks. Even his perfectly-gelled hairstyle appeared to have less product applied. Maybe I should have been concerned about his mental state but upon further reflection, the absence of color led me to believe he was merely attempting to work his way back into Charlie's good graces. At least his attire complimented the surroundings, meaning a global crisis had been temporarily averted.

Suddenly self-conscious, I looked down at my own clothing— boot-cut jeans, purple Chuck Taylor high-tops and a black Eddie Bauer Henley covered by a worn leather jacket—and wondered if Charlie would oust me for my inability to blend in with his environment. I chewed my lip as I noticed even Nicoh had me beat on that one, with his natural white, black and silver coat. Considering I was sporting my usual style, or lack thereof, perhaps Charlie had viewed Nicoh as my best accessory all along? I shrugged. There was nothing I could do about it now. Instead, I bit the bullet and attempted to make nice with Charlie's assistant.

"Hey Arch, it's great to see you."

Arch sniffed after taking in my appearance again and glanced disdainfully in Nicoh's direction before responding, "AJ, of all days you'd make Charlie wait on you, today is not that day." He pointed toward the atrium, then turned on his heel and marched off in the direction of the kitchen. Nice to know Arch hadn't changed much during his sabbatical.

Officially dismissed, I pulled Nicoh's mat from my bag and placed it in the area Charlie had designated "for the animal." Nicoh huffed as he grumpily climbed on and situated himself in the center. Once I was sure he was sufficiently comfortable, I scratched him behind the ears before making my way through the spacious penthouse—a study of glass and steel—with its luxurious open floor plan and modern industrial style. Charlie was strict with his color scheme, using only black and gray with an occasional white accent. The atrium was no different.

Charlie stood in the center of the seamless glass encapsulation —like a priceless treasure on display—though his current expression ruined that vision. A scowl formed as he perused the list on the iPad he clutched. I paused at the entrance, taking him in. He was tall and muscular yet lean, and impeccably dressed in a handsomely-tailored charcoal Armani suit and crisp white dress shirt that remained open at the neck. I was surprised by this last detail —Charlie was rarely without a tie—it was as casual as I had seen him since high school. His Berluti's tapped impatiently as he read. He was model attractive, a cross between Matt Bomer and Ian Somerhalder—though there had been speculation in the tabloids that the two actors had actually been separated at birth—with dark hair, striking gray-blue eyes, a strong angular jaw and cheekbones most women would die for. He was a sight, indeed.

Unfortunately, once he opened his mouth, the illusion was destroyed. Even with all his pretty-boy features, Charlie's personality and demeanor made him a less-than-likable human being. I wished I could say it was due to his privileged upbringing, but I had known his parents since we were children and they were everything he was not—kind, respectful, honest and above all else —generous.

Even Charlie's grandfather, a self-made software magnate and source of the family's substantial wealth and stature, had been a humble and gracious individual. Long after his passing, the senior Wilson had continued to leave his mark on our community through various charitable foundations. None of that had rubbed off on Charlie. Though he was smart and savvy, attending Harvard Business School and graduating with honors, he used all his privileges for his own arrogant, selfish gain.

A successful entrepreneur, he used his vast wealth to ruthlessly "collect" things and often took what others had acquired. When he was unable to do so to his liking, he simply one-upped them by obtaining something he felt was better than they had to offer. In the rare situations where he was unable to get what he wanted, he would throw legendary temper tantrums. And then, he'd get even.

Today, Charlie was in a wicked mood and just short of one of his tantrums. I noted his expression had grown a few shades blacker upon my arrival. On careful approach, I realized he had been reviewing the guest list, which I'd helped compile.

"What. Is. This?" he shouted, shaking the iPad at me.

For a moment, I was convinced his eyes would pop right out of his head. I chastised myself for thinking that might have been a blessing, if not so gruesome, as I gently removed the tablet from his clutches and glanced at the offending screen. It was *a* guest list, it just wasn't *the* guest list he and I had so painstakingly developed over the course of an entire weekend.

At the time, I remembered thinking he wouldn't be able to handle the intrusion of so many people in his home, but we managed to create a list of sixty-five close friends and business associates he claimed he felt comfortable with—meaning people who could actually stand to be in Charlie's presence for several hours and vice-versa. Before I had a chance to respond, he continued to rant, stabbing names on the list with his finger.

"*That* woman uses a self-tanner. I don't want that deposited all over my furniture." He wiped his brow feverishly from some imaginary perspiration before stabbing at another name. "*He* has the audacity to wear knock-off Gucci's, with tassels. Seriously, AJ, even in this economy, I just can't have it. And this guy—well, you dated him, so you are well aware—is a l-o-s-e-r." After squinting at the name beneath his manicured nail, I couldn't disagree, I had dated the loser back when we were in high school but again, Charlie didn't pause long enough for me to respond.

"Please explain, AJ, after all I have done for you, why have you chosen now to do this to me? Did you think I wouldn't notice this was not the guest list we discussed? That I would tolerate such…such disloyalty?" Though he was breathless, he was mid-boil, so there was no stopping him. "I just cannot believe you—of all people—would go behind my back and send out unapproved invites…to these…people. Are you…are you…trying to ruin me?" Finally, he paused for a moment, but not before delivering the final blow. "I fired Arch for lesser offenses," he spat, tossing the iPod to the ground and stomping his foot.

It took everything in me not to snicker at his outburst. He was as red as a grape tomato and as ridiculous-looking as a petulant child used to getting his way. Instead, I patiently waited for the blustering to subside before attempting to respond. After fifteen years, I had plenty of practice dealing with Charlie's outbursts and learned early on that laughing out loud—no matter how warranted it might be—was a bad idea. So I waited. And waited. And once Charlie appeared sufficiently calm—it typically took between three and five and half minutes, depending upon the circumstances—I finally spoke.

"Good morning, Charlie. Like the suit. While I have not had a chance to fully examine the list you are referencing, from the brief glimpse I did get, *that* is not the list you and I compiled and agreed upon, nor is it the one I sent the invitations from. If you would, quickly look at the dates. You will notice that—according to the date and time stamp on the document—the individuals you referenced were added days *after* you and I last met. Furthermore, I have not seen you or the list since that date." I ended on that note, thinking it seemed as though Arch might be getting a bit of revenge on Charlie for terminating his employment and then hiring him back in time to assist with the party.

I decided to let Charlie draw his own conclusions, which he did, considering the rate at which his face transformed into a menacing grimace. Before stalking off to find Arch, he barked out a few directions about the setup. I blew out a long breath, thinking I was off the hook, when he surprised me by spinning on his heel and looking me over from top to bottom. His mouth took a severe downward turn as he reached my worn purple Chucks.

"Make sure you and Leah dress appropriately this evening. It's called a White Party for a reason. I expect you to be dressed as though you were one of the guests." His eyes narrowed, warning me not to test him. Before I had the chance to weigh my options, he was gone.

* * *

Charlie had reluctantly decided to allow guests to have access to the entire penthouse during the party, though the atrium would serve as the focal point for the gathering. Considering my colorful comments about serving the other white meat—in an effort to stick with the whole white theme, of course—had been met with a look of repugnance only Charlie could muster, I wasn't surprised when he relegated me to overseeing the party's decor in lieu of assisting with the catering selections. Therefore, my task this morning was to make sure white touches were tastefully integrated into the existing surroundings as we'd previously discussed.

I was reminded of the party planning meeting, when Charlie had felt it necessary to inform me that "tasteful" did not include papier-mâché streamers, posterboard signs or balloons. Since that also ruled out clowns and face-painting, I had jokingly asked if ice sculptures would be acceptable, to which Charlie had tersely replied that was "so five years ago." Not to mention, completely unrealistic given the desert heat, though at the time, I doubted it had crossed Charlie's mind. It was about keeping up with the Jones', after all, or in this case, the Charlies.

In the end, it turned out that Charlie's main priority was to ensure the room photographed well. Having designed several of my own backdrops, using lighting, a few faux structures and gauzy materials, I was able to fabricate an environment that warmed the steel and glass by incorporating a light, airy feel, giving it an open and inviting ambiance, without making it look like a boudoir.

Several hours later, I realized I had managed to avoid a check-up visit from either Charlie or Arch. Surely Charlie didn't actually trust me, did he? Since my assigned tasks had been completed, I wasn't about to sit around pontificating, so I gathered my belongings and proceeded toward kitchen, where I could hear Arch yelling at the catering staff. I glanced around the corner, where a dozen workers scurried back and forth like crazed mice at Arch's direction, and noted that Charlie was nowhere to be found.

Sensing a break in Arch's diatribe, I quickly announced my presence before he resumed. His head swiveled ever so slightly upon hearing my voice, though he refused to make eye contact. Ignoring the slight, I gave him a quick update and indicated I would return in a few hours—prior to the start of the party and the arrival of the first round of guests—to photograph the penthouse. I also confirmed Leah would be in attendance to work the crowd and obtain choice tidbits to feed to the society rags, as Charlie had requested. Arch begrudgingly nodded, but did not offer Charlie's whereabouts.

Noting the time, I quickly collected Nicoh and drove home, hoping Leah had gotten her requisite hours of sleep. Anything less would result in a troublesome night and would most certainly get us both booted out of Charlie's party.

One could only hope.

CHAPTER TWO

Less than two hours later, Leah and I were dressed and back at Charlie's building. Before leaving, Nicoh had gotten his fill of scratches and snacks but was still miffed about being left behind. He demonstrated his irritation by positioning himself just within our line-of-sight as we exited, his backside facing us while he grumbled at some inanimate object in the opposite direction. Did I mention Alaskan Malamutes could also be moody and stubborn?

Not that I blamed him. If we could have opted-out of Charlie's party, we would have. We were both extremely uncomfortable in our appropriate—and very white—party attire, though Leah managed to look classy in her short, fitted cocktail dress and heels. Tiny rhinestone barrettes kept her cropped locks in place and framed her face, giving her an angelic halo effect.

I sighed as I tugged at my own ensemble, selected solely for the ease it allowed when lugging camera equipment around—tailored slacks with a matching suit jacket over a silk camisole, paired with short and strappy but still sensible sandals. I pulled my long dark hair into a high ponytail, leaving my bangs to hang freely. The only accent I afforded myself was on the lapel of my jacket, a circular diamond pin that had been my mother's.

"Stop fussing," Leah chastised as she drove, "you look fine." I fought the childish urge to stick my tongue out and instead pursed my lips in defiance, making her chuckle. "Someone's been spending too much time with Nicoh." This time we both laughed.

The rest of the trip was quiet. We had been friends long enough we no longer felt the need to fill the void with mundane chatter, though we were also aware the other had things to ponder.

Charlie was waiting for us as we entered the penthouse. We were ahead of schedule, but he operated on a different time zone than the rest of the modern world—the Charlie zone—where you were either always too early or too late, depending upon the circumstances. And Charlie's mood.

Before he spoke, he gave us both the once-over. While waiting for his approval, I returned the favor and checked out his duds. It was amazing me how a guy could pull off a completely white outfit, but Charlie managed to do so amazingly. His hair was carefully slicked back, adding to the effect, and suddenly I wondered if I was there to photograph the penthouse, or its owner?

Upon closer inspection, the only visible imperfections were the tiny black bags under his eyes. Thinking back to that morning, I hadn't recalled seeing them, though I'd been distracted by the incident with the invite list. Interesting, I thought to myself. It wasn't like Charlie to show physical signs of stress or fatigue. Oh sure, he demanded perfection—take this White Party, for example —but in the end, it was more to satisfy himself than to ensure the pleasure of others. No, obtaining the adoration of others was just the icing on the top of the Charlie cake. So what could be festering in that pretty little mind of his?

He might have been preoccupied, but he was also full of surprises. "You both look…satisfactory." Leah and I stole a glance at one another. Was that a compliment? From Charlie? Now I was convinced something was off, especially when he added, "You did a nice job with the atrium, AJ. It is quite lovely."

Before either of us could respond, Charlie strode toward kitchen, calling over his shoulder as he went, "We've got limited time before the guests start arriving. AJ, I suggest you start doing whatever it is you do. And you"—he shot a glance at Leah —"help her until you are needed elsewhere."

Now *that* was the Charlie I knew and loathed.

I had photographed Charlie's penthouse on several occasions —for magazine spreads, publicity ops and things of that nature— so I made quick work of setting up my equipment, as I was familiar with the type of images he required. Leah assisted me as needed, but otherwise sat quietly off to the side and watched—a little too quietly for Leah.

"Want to talk about it?" I asked, referring to the assignment that was most likely consuming her thoughts. "You've been awfully quiet since you handed your research off to Abe and Elijah."

She tilted her head and nodded, indicating she was still think-ing. "I know they hired me to do research—that I'm not investi-gating—but I think the gal disappeared for a reason and either doesn't want to be found, or—" her voice drifted off, her eyes sad.

"Or?" I gently prompted.

"Or can't be found." She sighed, brushing invisible bangs out of her eyes, before clasping her hands together tightly.

"You think she might be dead, then?"

"Yeah," her head bounced in agreement, "nothing in the research corroborates it, but…"

"But your gut says otherwise." Leah's hunches were often on the mark. Sadly, in this case, it would mean the parent's hope of finding their daughter alive, that she might one day come home, would be shattered.

I did my best to console my friend. "Either way, however this turns out, you have to know that Abe and Elijah will find her. They won't stop looking until they can provide the family some closure. You know that, right?" I knew my words offered little comfort, but I still wanted her to know she'd done all she could and Abe and Elijah would do the same.

Leah looked at me and nodded, her eyes brimming with tears. Finally, a small smile emerged. I hugged her gently—trying to avoid mussing her pretty dress—though she squeezed my hand in return, while wiping away an errant drop of moisture that had made its escape.

Leah started to speak just as Arch made his first appearance of the night, interrupting our moment and thankfully, our gloomy moods. I barely contained a giggle as I snuck a glance at Leah, realizing a moment too late I should have avoided doing so, because her perplexed expression made the situation even more hilarious as she repeatedly looked him over from head to toe. Arch was a condensed version of his boss, down to the last stitch. Even the gelled hair and spray tan had been cloned. But where Charlie had looked like…Charlie, Arch looked…well, let's just say it wasn't a good look.

Arch's eyes slivered as he took in our reception, aware we were working hard not to erupt with laughter.

He spoke, his tone clipped, "Charlie wants you"—looking in Leah's direction without making eye contact—"in the entry way. Now. You"—he swiveled his bobble head toward me—"need to wrap it up. The guests are arriving." On that note, he marched, very much like Charlie, right out of the atrium.

"Wow," was all Leah could muster before both of us broke out into shudders of raucous laughter. "Can you say twin-sy?" She started to laugh again but suddenly, her eyes grew wide and both hands flew to her mouth. "Oh…oh my…I'm so sorry AJ…I didn't mean…" I cut her off with a wave of my hand.

"It's ok." Reveling in the moment, she'd forgotten that I had once been a twin. "You should find Charlie before he and Arch have matching hissies." I looked at her, my smile genuine. She returned the smile, quickly squeezing my hand before leaving.

I worked in silence, tearing down the equipment before placing it in the spare closet as Charlie had instructed. I could hear several unfamiliar voices and realized Arch hadn't been exaggerating about guests arriving. Since Charlie had Leah off somewhere doing who knows what, I was on my own to smile and make polite small talk.

To his credit, Charlie had been wise to integrate Leah into the crowd. His parties were notorious for socializing, deal-brokering and of course, being seen. As a reporter, she had a knack for getting people to tell her the most interesting tidbits and though it wasn't her style to use the juicier morsels to further her career, it typically made for exciting popcorn nights.

I stood off to the edge of the atrium and took in the swarm of partygoers. Everyone dressed to impress in their finest white attire, which from my vantage point, made for an intriguing, if not outlandish scene. I'll openly admit I'm certainly no fashionista. My preferences tend to run toward the more classic styles as opposed to the latest, trendy ones favored this evening.

Just then, a statuesque chestnut-haired beauty glided toward Charlie, her movements effortless, as though her feet weren't touching the ground. I recognized her as one of his former girl-friends, Morgan Thompson. They surreptitiously air-kissed before engaging into mindless chatter. I was tall, but Morgan made me look puny. Her entrance made every head turn. Women sneered with envy while the men gawked with more lust than admiration. Her exotic beauty and physique were sure to make even the most breathtaking Victoria's Secret models feel self-conscious. And, as if her rocking bod and gorgeous features weren't devastating enough, the girl also had some serious brains to boot.

As a partner in a highly prestigious San Francisco law firm, Morgan was the whole package. How Charlie had managed to let her slip away was beyond me, though I suspected he brought more drama to a relationship than most girls were willing to accommodate, much less a catch like Morgan.

Like I said, she was a smart chick.

I was so engrossed watching the two interact, I belatedly realized another couple was heading my direction: Parker Harris and Natalie Ingram. I blanched inwardly, praying they would move beyond me. I was too late to stop, drop and roll right under one of Charlie's leather sofas, so I braced myself for the incoming assault.

Parker was one of Charlie's closest and oldest friends—as friends went in Charlie's realm—and Natalie was his girlfriend. We had all attended the same high school—Charlie, Parker, Leah and I—Natalie included, though she'd been a year behind the rest of us. Her brother, Greg, had been in our class and was the third spoke in Charlie and Parker's wheel when they all headed off to Harvard, though personally, I had always found him to be far too normal and way too nice to hang out with the other two. I never got their dynamic. And sadly, I never would.

A few years earlier, Greg had taken his own life. His death surprised everyone, including his two best friends. It was rumored he had been distraught over some failed business deals, but nothing substantial came out of it and neither Charlie nor Parker could lend any credence to the claim. In time, for everyone but Greg, life moved on.

An interesting side-effect of Greg's death came when Parker and Natalie starting dating. It was another union I would never understand. While Parker was competitive and often manipulative, Natalie was sweet and caring. Don't get me wrong, she was certainly no pushover and like Morgan, had brains to spare. Natalie, however, avoided the corporate workplace after graduating from the University of California at Berkeley, dedicating herself instead to charity work and causes that helped promote a better way of life for those who were less fortunate.

So no, I didn't understand her attraction to Parker. She was way too classy to put up with someone so self-involved. Perhaps the relationship allowed her a means of hanging on to a remnant of her brother's life? If that was the case, in my opinion, there were certainly far better ways of going about it.

As they approached, her honey-gold hair draped over her shoulders and down her back as though it were a silky shawl. She was the most tastefully dressed of this evening's attendees and could have passed for a modern day Audrey Hepburn in her white variation of the little black cocktail dress.

I bit my lip, tasting blood when I turned my gaze from Natalie to Parker and realized that, like Arch, he was dressed in exactly the same manner as Charlie. Except for his hairstyle, the twinsies had become triplets. While Charlie and Arch had chosen a slick coif for the evening's festivities, Parker retained his usual perfected bedhead look. Rather than proceeding to make hamburger of my lip, I kept my snickering at bay by reflecting on the similarities between the two friends.

Parker was tall, lean, and modestly handsome and like his pal, Charlie, once his mouth opened, all admiration quickly fell away. But if anyone could exceed Charlie's haughty, self-important demeanor, it was Parker.

"Ariel," he chirped.

Even though we had known each other for years, he purposefully slighted me at any given opportunity, erroneously calling me by one name or the other. I could only assume he'd been watching *The Little Mermaid* before the party. Natalie looked embarrassed and quietly corrected him, though they were standing close enough I heard the exchange.

He shushed her before continuing, his words slurring with

drink, "I heard you were attempting to fill Arch's shoes after he was ousted from his stoop."

Natalie gave me an apologetic glance. Parker was in one of his more antagonistic moods and trying to bait me into an argument. Under other circumstances, I would have welcomed it. Tonight, I was technically on duty, so I complimented Natalie on her lovely dress instead.

Leah must have sensed the incoming attack—or had just seen Parker's beeline in my direction—because suddenly she was at my side, giving Parker a whole new focus, which unfortunately was directed right at her chest.

"Natalie! Parker!" she exclaimed with as much enthusiasm as she could muster. "It's so great to see you. Natalie, hon, you look divine. Doesn't she, Parker?" she gritted out in an attempt to divert his attention back to his girlfriend, who reddened as he continued to ogle my friend.

Leah was having none of it. "You look good, too, Parker. In fact, you and Charlie could be twinsies. Did you two call each other to coordinate? And was that before or after he called Arch?" She giggled slyly as she casually pointed to where Arch was talking animatedly to several of Charlie's guests.

Natalie let a giggle of her own slip as she took in Parker's exasperated look. It was obvious neither she nor Parker had known Arch had been reinstated as Charlie's assistant, much less known he'd be present this evening. His being dressed similarly to Charlie was like adding sprinkles to a platter filled with cupcakes.

Parker attempted to redeem himself, his eyes finally detaching themselves from Leah's breasts. "Lulu, you wouldn't know taste if it—"

Natalie interrupted him before he was able to finish that thought, "Parker, we should say hello to the congressman." She smiled as she not-so-gently tugged his arm and used the bulk of her small frame to propel him forward.

Parker obliged but muttered something under his breath that I won't repeat. As they departed, Natalie shot us a quick wink over her right shoulder. I marveled at her diplomacy and her ability to successfully avert a nasty altercation within the first hour of the party. The girl definitely had more grit than I'd initially given her credit for.

"Thanks for the save, who knows what would have come out of my mouth," I admitted ruefully as I turned to Leah.

"I know," she laughed, clearly pleased, "it was almost a shame to stop you. He deserved whatever it was you were going to unleash on him. I just don't get what Natalie sees in him. Dating Parker takes her IQ down a few digits in my book." I nodded but Natalie's actions as of late had me wondering.

I directed my attention back to my friend. "What the heck have you been up to?"

"Charlie's had me working the room like I was a hooker down on Van Buren Street." Ugh, and here I'd thought I'd had a rough night thus far. "He wanted me to make nicey-nice with a few of his new investor buddies, but that didn't include complimentary grabs of my front or backside, so I moved on. Anyway, I just got done talking to our newest congressman, Bob Fenton. Interesting fellow." She nodded toward a short, cherubic-looking kid clinking martini glasses with Parker, while laughing at something that had been said.

"Uh, *he's* a congressman?" I gasped. "What is he, like twelve?"

Leah chuckled. "Something like that. He's actually got some fresh ideas and a lot of positive energy. I'll be interested to see how he does in the months to come."

I nodded absently, not interested in discussing the new

congressman's political ambitions, as something distinctly more intriguing had caught my eye. Leah stopped to follow my gaze.

Natalie continued talking to Congressman Fenton as Parker turned to catch Charlie's attention before he left the room. Hearing Parker call out, Charlie attempted to retreat in the opposite direction. Parker, however, anticipated the move, hastily stepping close enough to latch onto Charlie's arm. The sounds of the party drowned out their brief conversation, but body language left nothing to the imagination. Charlie barely glanced at his friend, anger flaring in his eyes as he snatched his arm away, leaving Parker to scowl. As quickly as Charlie's anger manifested, it was gone the instant he began talking to the next partygoer.

Natalie also witnessed the interaction and as Parker's outstretched hand turned into a fist, ended her conversation with the congressman and moved to grasp it in almost a dance-like motion, forcing his attention away from Charlie and onto her. Parker rolled her into his arms, smiling tightly as he kissed her forehead, though his eyes remained on his friend. Natalie touched his chin, then ushered him out of the atrium. If Charlie sensed their departure, he made no visible acknowledgment. Obviously something was up between the two besties, though I doubted anyone else had seen the altercation.

It was the first and only interesting point for the remainder of the evening. We didn't see Parker or Natalie again, which actually wasn't all that unusual, given the size of the penthouse and the sheer volume of the people milling about. Everyone seemed to be enjoying themselves, though it likely had more to do with the heavy handed bartender mixing drinks than anything else. Fortunately, due to the limited parking surrounding the building, many of the guests had already planned to take taxis both to and from the party, hopefully ensuring everyone made it home safely.

In the meantime, Leah and I sipped club soda as she introduced me to several partygoers, which included Congressman

Fenton, former State Senator Davis Conrad, a few local musicians, an aspiring L.A. fashion consultant and the architect who designed the building. Though I wasn't surprised Leah knew them, it was shocking Charlie had so many famous friends.

Speaking of Charlie, we finally ran into him again in the wee hours of the morning, as the party was winding down and were pleasantly surprised when he announced we were free to leave. I was curious about his sudden graciousness but didn't wait around, being way too familiar with his propensity for changing his mind.

Leah and I spent the ride home quietly thinking about the altercation between Charlie and Parker, though neither of us mentioned it. Something about the evening had been bothering me, but the minute we arrived home and I freed a few of the covers from beneath Nicoh's snoring form, that train went right on down the tracks just as soon as my head hit the pillow.

CHAPTER THREE

Despite exhaustion, the nightmares continued to plague me. Images flickered like an old black and white film reel, each frame more horrific than the last. Had there been even a splash of color, it would have been red. Crimson. The fear was unbearable, though some invisible force stifled my screams. Death presented himself, tall and imposing. Except for his face, masked by the shadows, I could distinguish every detail about him, down to the stitching on his jacket. I reached out in an attempt to wipe away the haze that concealed his features, but his identity was not for to me to know. "Not this time," came the whisper, just as a chill riveted my body, waking me.

I cursed the buzzing in my head as my eyes adjusted to the sun peeking through the blinds. I was still groggy from sleep, so it took me a moment to register the annoyance as an incoming text message on my cell phone, which I had carelessly placed beside my pillow when I had fallen into bed. Thanks to my fitful slumber, it was now buried—under Nicoh. I wrinkled my nose in disgust as a carefully extracted it, noting it was covered with drool.

I had only received one text message during the short time I had been home, from an unavailable source. *ITS TIME ARIANNA* was all it said. *Time for what?* I wondered. Time to get up, brush my teeth and start working? I didn't need a reminder for that. My curiosity about the message dissolved when Leah burst into my room, her hair wild and eyes raccoony, a side-effect of the previous night's makeup.

Before I had a chance to make a snarky comment, she breathlessly cried out "Parker is missing!" before flopping down on the corner of the bed—the only space available—given that Nicoh was still monopolizing the majority of the queen-sized mattress. She looked at me, her eyes wide and nearly as crazy as the tangled spikes sprouting out of her head.

"What do you mean he's 'missing'?"

Before she could answer, Nicoh let out a disgusted snort before jumping off the bed—apparently we weren't respecting his beauty sleep—leaving us in search of a quieter, less crowded resting place.

"Natalie went to check on Parker this morning and when she noticed his car was gone, figured he'd taken a taxi home from the party. After ringing the doorbell several times and receiving no response, she let herself in with her key. There was no indication that he'd slept in his bed or even made it home. She then called Charlie, who discovered that Parker's Audi was still parked several blocks from his building—it had actually been ticketed. After checking around with some of Parker's other friends and having no luck, she decided to contact the Tempe Police Department to report him missing."

"Let me get this straight. Natalie and Parker came to the party —separately?"

Leah nodded. "Natalie was at a charity event before the party, so they agreed to meet at Charlie's. In fact, she arrived before

Parker and ended up waiting for him in the foyer so they could ride the elevator up together."

"And when they left?"

"Parker called Natalie a cab, they said their goodbyes and she left. That was the last time she saw him."

"What about Charlie? Did Parker go back up to the party?"

"No, Charlie never saw Parker again that night. Claims he never saw him after—well, after that altercation we witnessed—though he describes it a bit differently. The doorman also said Parker never went back into the building. Of course, they haven't checked the security cameras or anything like that yet to confirm it."

"Security cameras of the building's entrance?"

"Yes, those too, but Charlie had cameras installed inside the penthouse before the party."

Cameras *inside* the penthouse? That was news to me, though not all that surprising, given Charlie's disposition. I was more surprised he hadn't installed them during the initial construction of the building, considering he owned it. Then again, perhaps Charlie decided to have them installed because of Arch's return, in case Arch decided to retaliate for being fired in the first place. Now *that* sounded more like the Charlie we all knew and endured. Something else occurred to me.

"How exactly did you get all this information, anyway?"

Leah shrugged. "Except for the part about the penthouse cameras, which Charlie accidentally let slip the other day, a friend at the Tempe Police Department clued me in on the rest. He remembered I'd gone to school with Parker and knew I'd been at the same party last night, so he called after Natalie reported him missing."

"What friend is this?"

"Just someone I met back when I was still working the crime beat at the paper. He might have developed a bit of a crush on me

—the feeling wasn't mutual—but he still feeds me info now and then."

"Hmm, must have been more than a crush." I wiggled my eyebrows suggestively but Leah snorted. "How do we know Parker didn't just ditch Natalie so he could hit one of the nearby clubs? He's probably sleeping off a hangover at some random chick's place. No disrespect to Natalie, but Parker *is* Parker."

"At this point, no one knows anything for sure, but in the meantime…" she paused, scrunching her face in preparation for my reaction, "Natalie wants us to form a search party."

"A what? You have got to be kidding me."

Leah shook her head. "Somehow Natalie managed to convince Charlie it was a good idea and something to do while we wait for TPD to do their thing. She probably pulled the Parker-would-do-the-same-if-the-situation-was-reversed card, though given the display last night, I'd be surprised if Charlie would fall for that alone. Anyway, she wants us to start looking around the area for clues or anything that could lead to Parker's whereabouts, at least until the police get more involved."

"Hold up." I raised a hand. "What is this 'we' and 'us' business? Parker's not even our friend. We don't know his habits." Nor did I want to.

"The thing is…" Leah sighed, "Natalie asked for our help. She called me, filled me in on a few details my TPD friend hadn't provided and I ended up feeling kinda bad for her. It's just a few hours and the least we can do to ease her mind."

I nodded, Natalie was a sweet girl. I hated to think what she was going through. I was going to be angry when Parker finally showed up and shattered whatever illusion she had about their relationship.

"And if we end up finding out Parker was on a bender, or out conjugating irregular verbs with some other gal?"

"Then we let the chips fall," Leah replied solemnly.

"Promise?"

"Promise. And one more thing?"

"What?" I asked cautiously.

Leah squirmed, something that was uncharacteristic for her. *Uh oh,* I thought. "Um, Charlie suggested you bring 'the dog' with you—his phrase, not mine." I could only assume Charlie had conveniently mistaken Nicoh, an Alaskan Malamute, with a Bloodhound.

I shook my head—it was going to be a long day.

* * *

We joined Charlie, Arch and Natalie outside the building an hour later. Nicoh ignored Charlie and Arch but immediately took to Natalie, sticking his nose into parts unknown in an effort to get acquainted. I swear, sometimes having an Alaskan Malamute can be so embarrassing.

"Nicoh!" I cried, horrified I had failed to get a handle on him before he managed to insinuate himself onto the new girl. Fortunately, Natalie laughed as she bent down to scratch Nicoh's ears, nuzzling his face with her own.

"It's ok. We had Labrador Retrievers growing up—they were mostly Greg's dogs—but they preferred my bed at night, so I'm used to the intrusion."

Relieved by her response, though still appalled by Nicoh's behavior, I chuckled. "Yeah, I know how that goes."

She nodded and laughed, flipping Nicoh's tail. Excited to have a new playmate, Nicoh scrunched down on his front legs—his behind still wagging in the air—before leaping onto all fours and whisking himself into a series of circles in an attempt to catch his tail. Soon, he had Leah, Natalie and me laughing, causing him to whoo-whoo with delight. Charlie, meanwhile, tapped his foot impatiently while Arch looked bored. Not satisfied with getting attention from only half the crowd, Nicoh attempted the feat again, this time a little too close for the guys' comfort, as they quickly shuffled to put some distance between themselves and the frenzied canine.

I stifled a chuckle. "No worries, guys. Nicoh only goes after things he finds interesting." The looks I received told me they were clearly not amused.

For a moment, the distraction almost made us forget the reason we had gathered at this unforgivable hour of the morning. We hadn't even had a chance to get our caffeinated kickstarter yet.

As if reading my mind, Natalie moved to a tray that had been sitting behind us on a retaining wall and carefully lifted out delicious-smelling coffee beverages, handing each of us one. Ah, liquid gold, I thought as I happily drank in the elixir, nodding my approval to Leah. Natalie was definitely a keeper.

Once everyone was satisfactorily charged, Leah turned to Charlie, "So what's the plan, Stan? Where is everybody?"

At his open-mouthed, surprised look, Natalie quickly stepped in, "Um, this is it. We are the search party. I couldn't get a hold of any of Parker's other friends, so we're it."

Charlie pursed his lips while Arch scoffed—this had clearly been Natalie's idea—and while neither of them thought Parker was missing, they didn't want to have to tell Natalie their suspicions about his current location. I shook my head at him to confirm he would keep his mouth shut. When he glared in return, Leah drew a line across her throat in warning and received a nasty look of her own.

Oblivious to the unspoken conversation among the rest of us, Natalie prattled on, "It's probably better if we start small anyway. At least it will be easier to coordinate our efforts, until the police get involved. I was thinking Charlie and Arch could walk the grounds surrounding the building, then the area where his car was parked."

"Where is Parker's car?" Leah asked.

"We had to move it," Natalie replied. "The City of Tempe was about to tow it, so Charlie, Arch and I took care of it before you arrived. There wasn't anything out of the ordinary in it," she added, before continuing with her plan.

"While the guys go in that direction, I thought the three of us… oh, sorry Nicoh," she smiled down at her new friend, his body resting across her feet, "make that four of us, could walk along the portion of the lake that borders the building." She pointed in the direction she had referenced, just 500 feet from where we were currently standing.

Charlie snorted in amusement. "You think Parker…what? Decided to go for a little late night dip in Tempe Town Lake?"

I grimaced at the nastiness in his tone. He was on the brink of putting the kibosh on the whole outing, meaning he was also on the verge of telling Natalie his thoughts on the whereabouts of her missing boyfriend.

Before he had a chance to continue, I quickly stepped in, "Natalie's right. Perhaps Parker wanted to clear his head before going home, so he took a brief walk along the pathway. Your bartender was pouring some pretty stiff drinks, Charlie."

To my relief, everyone nodded in agreement—except Charlie, of course—it seemed plausible.

"She's right," Leah added. "I saw Parker order about a half dozen gin and tonics…and that was early on in the evening."

Natalie sighed, clearly disappointed Parker had been seen imbibing so heavily at the White Party, but I could see my diversion had worked. The focus was now off Charlie's big mouth. "Actually, it was five—five gin and tonics—though all were pretty light on the tonic."

"Whatever," Charlie grumbled, rolling his eyes, "can we get

this show on the road?" Without waiting for an answer, he stalked in the direction of where I assumed Parker's car had been located. Arch shot a glance in our direction, his expression undecipherable, before faithfully scooting off after his boss.

Leah clapped her hands. "Shall we, girls…and pooch?"

The four of us proceeded in the direction of the lake's walking path. It was starting to get warm, so I was glad everyone had chosen the appropriate attire for the outing.

Once we reached the pathway, Natalie piped up, "I think we should split up. You two could maybe take Nicoh and head west on the path, toward Tempe Beach Park and I'll head east toward Scottsdale Road, though I probably won't go quite that far. If we could just find…anything…" her voice trailed off as her eyes filled with tears.

I looked to Leah for assistance. Perhaps it would be better to tell her what everyone was thinking—that Parker was probably sleeping off a bender somewhere? Wouldn't it be more humane than putting her through all this agony?

Before either of us could respond, Natalie wiped her eyes and smiled thinly. "Anyway, does the divide and conquer plan work for the two of you?"

We gave her the thumbs up and she marched east, but not before giving us a quick wave and a confident nod of the head.

As Leah, Nicoh and I started west—not exactly sure what we were looking for—I reflected on Natalie varied temperaments. "She seems younger than she is, don't you think? Fragile at times, stronger at others."

"Yeah," Leah replied, "I think Greg's death affects her more than most people realize. Greg was her big brother. Her rock. Her protector. Professionally, she appears strong, especially when it comes to her philanthropic endeavors, but in her personal life— just look how she's latched onto her brother's best friend," she commented, mirroring my own thoughts. "Who, by the way, is totally not right for her."

I agreed with her and said as much, "Natalie definitely deserves a lot better. Do you think she is trying to hold onto whatever memory is left of her brother?"

Leah nodded. "Seems like a pretty tortuous way of going about it, if you ask me."

We walked for a distance in silence, still not sure what we were doing, but out of concern for Natalie, we proceeded to look for clues indicating Parker had drifted this way. Eww, poor choice of words, though I'll admit, I did find myself peering into the lake, just to be sure. The three of us continued to walk the path, stopping occasionally to let Nicoh sniff. A lot of people brought their dogs along this route, so there were plenty of scents to keep him entertained. I doubt we had gotten more than a mile when my cell phone starting ringing—Natalie.

She was breathless, her usually soft voice coming across the connection in a half-screech, "I think I found something! Can you…can you come back?"

"Stay put," I commanded, though—silly me—I doubted she would go running off, "we're on our way." Again, unnecessary, though hopefully knowing we were coming would prevent her from completely losing it.

By jogging we were able to reach her more quickly than we would have had we walked, but looking at her face once we arrived, it had clearly seemed like an eternity from her perspective. I surveyed the surroundings, noting Natalie had made it farther east than I would have imagined. She stood rigidly, hugging herself with both arms, her eyes wild. In her hot pink running ensemble, she looked like a piece of bubblegum, ready to explode.

She shakily pointed to her finding. It was a white tie, much like the one many of the men, including Arch, Charlie and Parker, had been sporting the prior evening. Now smudged with dirt and grime and hopelessly crinkled, it trailed limply down the embankment.

While Leah and I peered at it, Natalie nervously uttered, "There's more."

She pointed, this time a few feet down from where we were standing. A man's white Berluti shoe sat on the edge of the dirt pathway, threatening to tumble into the crisp lake water. Like the tie, it was filthy and scuffed, though I knew the prior evening, it had been new.

Natalie rooted around in her large designer bag—an odd choice given the occasion—in an attempt to muffle the sniffles she had been fighting. As she finally extracted a tissue, they turned to guttural, heart-wrenching sobs. Leah and I quickly moved in to console her.

"They're his!" she cried, her voice filled with despair as she leaned her tiny frame into us.

I nodded to Leah—it was time to call the police. We, too, could not deny that Parker could have worn the tie and shoe the previous night. It was too much of a coincidence, especially considering neither Charlie nor Arch would have ambled along this pathway under any circumstances, much less after the party. No, unless there had been another partygoer wearing the same items, they likely belonged to Parker.

Leah stepped away to make the call, while Natalie clutched me tightly. Even Nicoh could sense the gravity of the situation and whoo-whoo'd quietly as I firmly held his lead to prevent him from sniffing the evidence.

A few moments later Leah returned to tell us the police would be sending a team out to our location shortly. "They'd like us to stay put and refrain from touching anything. You didn't, did you, Natalie?" The girl's eye widened as she shook her head from side to side. "While we wait for TPD to arrive then, I should probably call Charlie."

When they joined us a short while later, Charlie and Arch had found nothing of merit in their search for Parker, though given the enormous cones each was carrying, it was obvious they had managed to locate a new gelato shop. At our disgusted expressions, Charlie merely shrugged and indicated that technically, the shop had been in the vicinity of where Parker's car had been parked.

Leah and I shook our heads while Natalie—in a strange twist —threw herself into Charlie's arms. Apparently, his side adventure didn't bother her. The unexpected embrace, however, caught Charlie off-guard, forcing him to quickly adjust his balance. Seeing Charlie's attempt to maneuver triple scoops would have been comical had the circumstances not been so serious. Instead, he quickly shoved the cone at Arch while throwing him a frosty warning. I suspected Arch already knew better than to drop Charlie's treat, even though he had his own triple threat to contend with. I shook my head, wondering if these two possessed the capacity to understand the gravity of the situation. If it meant having to put their own needs aside for the sake of Parker's, then I highly doubted it.

Charlie managed to look interested as Natalie animatedly retraced her steps and pointed at her findings. Once finished, she crumpled against him and started to sniffle into his shirt. Charlie hastily moved her away, making it appear as though he wanted to look at her as he spoke. Knowing better, I glanced at Leah, who mouthed "silk."

To my surprise, he spoke to her into the softest, gentlest voice I had ever heard him use, "You will have to tell all of this to the police when they arrive."

If he had thought this would keep the girl from ruining his shirt, his plan backfired as she gripped him even more closely and openly sobbed. This time, Charlie looked as though he too, wanted to cry.

Fortunately, two black and white patrol units rolled up, saving us from having to witness that particular display. A pair of officers exited each cruiser—one male team and one male and female —the latter approached us as the prior surveyed the scene.

While Natalie relayed her story to the female officer, her male counterpart asked Leah and me to do the same. I rolled my eyes when Leah's flirtatious streak reared its ugly head as she told the officer his outfit looked cute. Ladies—for future reference— never, ever refer to a man's clothing as an "outfit" or "cute." I'm warning you—just don't do it.

Before the officer could arrest her, I stepped in with my own responses, which seemed to mollify the situation as he loosened his stance, even bending down to give Nicoh a healthy round of scratches. He then surprised me by asking if Nicoh had ever had any police dog training. I told him no, not to my knowledge, though some of Nicoh's previous background was unknown. I went on to tell him Nicoh certainly didn't retain any of the training I had taken him to, which likely had more to do with owner error than Nicoh's ability. The officer laughed, noting that he had previously had a canine partner.

Of course, Leah couldn't resist the chance to pipe up. "I'll bet your partner was the better driver."

Having finally gotten the attention off her flirtations, I winced, convinced there were handcuffs in both of our futures if she didn't let up soon. Thankfully, the officer chuckled this time.

"Is this enough evidence to consider Parker a missing person? His girlfriend, Natalie"—I gestured in the direction where Natalie was still talking to the female officer—"can verify he was wearing a similar tie and pair of shoes last night, while Charlie and Arch can confirm the two items aren't theirs, since they were all wearing the same attire last night." The officer was vague in his response but took the information down before excusing himself.

A short time later, a crime scene unit arrived and technicians began collecting evidence from the area cordoned off by the two male officers. It was a little too reminiscent of the scene in my alley a few months earlier, when I had discovered a body in my dumpster, who as it later turned out, belonged to my sister. At least there wasn't a body today, I shuddered. Though I was no fan of Parker's, I held out hope he would make an appearance soon.

The hours that followed were a blur. The effects of the coffee had long worn off and now adrenaline kept me in an upright position. Even Nicoh napped at my side, a few snores escaping every so often. Only he could sleep so soundly in the middle of such commotion, I thought, a bit jealously. Finally, one of the officers told us we were free to go, indicating we would be contacted if there were additional questions. I wondered if perhaps they too thought Parker was sleeping off a hangover somewhere.

Leah and I said goodbye to Charlie and Arch and confirmed they would keep an eye on Natalie as she traipsed after the investigators, begging for information. Though the female officer had done a good job of appeasing the girl, it was all she could do to keep Natalie from insinuating herself into their investigation.

"Maybe now is a good time to contact Ramirez?" Leah suggested.

Overhearing her, the female officer suddenly turned. "Ramirez? As in Phoenix Homicide Detective Jonah Ramirez?"

"Yeah, he's a friend of ours. You know him?" Leah replied.

I swore the officer nearly licked her lips. "Oh yeah, I know him," her voice was lustful as she returned to her duties, leaving us to stare after her. My eyes shot daggers at her back until Nicoh whimpered quietly, forcing Leah to tug my sleeve. I realized I had been gripping the scruff of his neck a little too fiercely.

"Sorry," I mumbled to both of them, glancing over my

shoulder one last time in the officer's direction. "For a minute, I thought I was going to have to take her." As I turned to join my friend, I was pretty sure I heard a muffled giggle escape from behind me.

I grimaced and wished the day could just be over already.

CHAPTER FOUR

Of course, my genie failed me and my wish never came true. Despite the pleasant weather we had during our impromptu search, the clouds rapidly rolled in from the west and threatened the official search party's efforts, which was well under way by the time we departed. We took turns calling the police department for updates, but nothing more had been found. After several hours of combing the area surrounding the lake for clues, divers had been sent into the lake. Everyone was still holding out hope Parker would return on his own but as time passed, it became less and less likely.

Against our pleas, Natalie insisted upon camping out at his house to wait, refusing offers to keep her company. In many ways, she was more resilient than we had initially given her credit for, now that the shock of Parker's disappearance had become more of a reality. Still, Leah and I felt a certain amount of protectiveness toward her, knowing that somewhere beneath her current tough girl facade, the fragile one still remained.

I wasn't familiar with the requirements for searching a man-made body of water such as Tempe Town Lake with inflatable dams at either end, but as it turned out, it wasn't much easier than doing so in a natural body of water. Dirt, sediment and other various odds and ends still shifted and moved with the current, often serving as barriers to the diver's efforts. Of course, the constant threat of the impending monsoon didn't help the weather. We'd had an unusually wet spring as well, which was good for ensuring the summer months would have enough moisture to withstand a tempestuous fire season, but bad for locating clues within a muck-filled basin.

The days were gray and at any given moment, light quickly dissolved into darkness, ending the day's search efforts. In the meantime, Leah and I kept ourselves occupied with work. She juggled a few freelance article requests with her research for Abe and Elijah while I shuttled between photo shoots.

Fortunately, my contracts were for inside work, which wasn't always the case. I also got to test some tasty snacks from the new tapas restaurant on 5th Avenue in Old Town Scottsdale whose owner had hired me to shoot their interior and several menu items for use on their website and in local magazines.

My next photo shoot was at a West Phoenix resort and casino that had recently renovated and needed new marketing materials for an upcoming advertising campaign, followed by a third for a gallery association in Central Phoenix. Each project was interesting in its own right and would certainly be useful for obtaining future work, but my mind wandered as I obsessed about Parker.

Three days later, the storm finally broke free. The sky turned blacker than night and wind taunted the trees, whipping them back and forth like matchsticks. Lightning filled the sky, the tips lashing out and crackling before touching down in fiery anger. Thunder followed its belligerent friend, booming and bellowing in lightning's wake. Then came the rain. The first drops teased the ground as if testing its surface. Growing impatient, it spilled in rivulets, panes of water drenching anything within reach. The wind provided an additional burst of energy and the elements mingled in their theatrical dance. Roads became impassable due to fallen trees and surface streets transitioned from running streams to treacherous, overflowing roadways. The monsoon was upon us. Despite its baffling interplay, it also provided something more—movement. Movement of objects that had been lodged, stagnant and stymied without the benefit of the natural ebb and flow, now brought forth from their silent slumber. Murky water cleared the path as branches and debris broke free from their watery graves.

Parker Harris became one of these objects. His body, now a contorted, bloated mass, had been tangled in the disarray, remaining at the lake's mercy until the storm released him from his temporary resting place. When the storm passed and the divers were able to resume their search, they found him lodged against an embankment, just east of where we had ended our own search.

Using her press credentials and TPD source, Leah had managed to work her way onto the scene at the lake and was gathering details here and there while whispering them to me via cell phone. We both knew the body retrieved from the lake was Parker's, even though the Maricopa County Medical Examiner's Office would officially confirm his identity after conducting their own investigation and medical examination. For us, the facts surrounding his disappearance made the truth inevitable.

None of Charlie's other party guests had gone missing and according to the scuttlebutt at scene, the body was still partially-clothed in a white dress shirt, white suit pants and one very white, very expensive-looking dress shoe. It had yet to be identified as a mate to the Berluti Natalie had found, but it was quite a coincidence.

Leah also gathered other details that weren't so expected. Rumblings about trauma and unusual wound patterns were tossed about, but to her frustration—as verified by the variety of new curse words she uttered in my ear—nothing would be confirmed until the Medical Examiner's inquest.

Our conversation was interrupted by an incoming text message, likely from Charlie, so I placed her on hold while I read it. *IM COMING* was all it said. Again, the sender was unavailable. With the drama surrounding Parker's disappearance, I had completely forgotten about the previous text. Was it from the same person? I shrugged, though it was annoying, the message was probably harmless. I returned to my conversation with Leah and found her cussing me out.

"What the heck, Leah?"

"Err…oh good, you're back! I'm totally freaking out here and was about to pull every hair out of my head!"

"What hair?" I quipped.

"I'm being serious here, Ajax!" That got my attention. "When they were hauling the body out of the lake, one of the technicians slipped and the stretcher slid sideways," she paused to catch her breath, "causing the tarp to shift, exposing—"

"Ewww, I don't want to hear this!"

Leah quickly interjected, "No, it only slipped a little, off one foot. There was no shoe or sock, and that's when I saw it!"

"What? What did you see?"

I heard her expel a deep breath. "Despite being all…all bloaty, there was a scar," she paused a moment to let out another extended breath. "It started at the left side of the ankle and ran in a jagged pattern across the foot, ending at the big toe."

I gasped. I had seen a marking just as Leah described, years earlier. First, in its fresh, bloodied wound state and again, months later when it had healed into an ugly, fleshy scar. In fact, I had been present when the jerk it belonged to had gotten handsy with a particularly spunky little blonde. After his ungentlemanly attempts at pawing her lady parts, she had swiftly—and quite impressively—dispatched a red stiletto into his sandaled foot. The perpetrator had howled like a wounded moose and after removing his offensive mitts, attempted to free his foot from the spiky heel still embedded in the soft tissue. The sudden movement ripped and tore the skin in a jagged motion, all the way down to the big piggy toe. The would-be perpetrator had limped away, humiliated, after receiving the penance he deserved for his unwelcomed, unsavory actions.

Over the years, the recollections of the incident became increasingly grandiose, as tales tend to do. Every detail, every nuance was more animated from one telling to the next, until its notoriety became so far-reaching people began telling me about the perky little blonde who had bruised more than the ego of the well-known playboy. She had scarred him—permanently.

Looking back, I had enjoyed that particular memory. Now, I would have done anything to erase the image of the day Leah had left her mark on Parker Harris.

CHAPTER FIVE

We didn't need an autopsy to confirm the body was Parker's. We did, however, need answers about how he had died and more importantly, ended up in the lake. If not for Parker, then for the people he'd left behind. Like Natalie.

She had several of her own connections and was likely aware a body had been found. Not wanting her to be alone in Parker's house, Leah picked me up after leaving the scene so we could check on her. On our way, we debated about divulging our suspicions. We didn't have definitive DNA proof but the scar was, in our minds, almost proof enough. Besides, it would be weeks before the Medical Examiner's report was released and forcing her to wait any longer might be too much, considering her fluctuating emotional state.

As we approached the towering Spanish-style villa where Parker had lived, Natalie threw the door open, as though expecting our arrival, and hugged us both fiercely. When she finally pulled away, her eyes were red from extensive crying and she seemed thinner than I remembered her being. Clearly, Parker's disappearance was taking its toll.

After guiding us through the maze of a house, she selected a room with the most comfortable couches and once settled, we gently told her what Leah had witnessed, bracing for an eruption of emotion. To our surprise, several moments of silence later, the waterworks still hadn't broken through. I spared a glance at Leah, but my friend's expression told me she had no more idea than I did. Finally, Natalie slowly lifted her head, her eyes free of tears, and simply nodded.

"Thank you for caring enough to tell me the truth. Based upon your description, I think it's him, too. At least now I know." She sighed, then rose from her seated position and gestured toward the door. "I don't mean to seem rude, or unappreciative, but I'd like to be alone now. I need to remember Greg as he was. When I last saw him." On that note, she shuffled out of the room and down the hall, leaving us both wide-eyed and somewhat stupefied.

"She just said—" Before Leah could continue, I quickly put my finger to my lips and motioned to the door. She nodded, taking my cue as we quietly let ourselves out.

Safely out of earshot, she excitedly whispered, "Natalie called Parker by her brother's name!"

I nodded. "She must be in shock. Did you notice how she didn't show any emotion when we told her about the scar?"

"I know it, and after all that huggy-feely crap with Charlie the other day, too! What the heck was that all about? And now, she's got nothing?"

"I'm more concerned about leaving her alone in that house than I am about her emotions being all over the map."

"I don't feel great about leaving her either, but she asked us to let her have some time to herself. Perhaps we should do as she asks, then check on her later?" Leah suggested.

I agreed and as we made our way to her car, I glanced back at Parker's house, my thoughts of the girl suffering inside. Something told me Natalie was battling more than the shock of losing Parker. His death had likely resurrected the demons of her past.

Something I was all too familiar with. It made me wonder how any of us managed to survive, how we got through each day and got up to tackle the next. As we pulled away, I looked at Leah and thought of Nicoh, and had my answer. My thoughts returned to Natalie—who or what would be hers?

Only time would tell. I hoped she could hold out for that long, before the demons destroyed her forever.

* * *

On our way home, Leah surprised me by asking if I had planned on calling Ramirez. Ah, Jonah Ramirez—tall, dark and a mystery in and of himself. The homicide detective and I had gotten acquainted when my sister had been murdered several months earlier, but once the case had been closed—meaning the perps had been handed off to the FBI—the detective and I had developed a friendship of sorts. The kind where we'd had several lunches and dinners together, gone on a few day trips to Sedona, Oak Creek Canyon and Tucson with Nicoh and even attended a few local art and music festivals. But aside from a few moon-hanging kisses, I wasn't exactly sure where we stood.

I got the distinct impression he liked me. I definitely liked him and though I hadn't quite managed to make a fool out of myself yet, had planted a few of my own jaw-dropping smooches on him. Anyway, I was pretty sure he knew I liked him, too.

Still, there were times he seemed to be filled with sadness and even a bit of regret, which led me to believe perhaps he wasn't quite over a former lady love, though she hadn't been the topic of conversation to date. As confusing as that made things, I enjoyed his company and let him take the lead, going at a pace he felt comfortable. I wasn't going anywhere and well, he was certainly worth the wait, however long that might be.

Leah snapped me out of my reverie, "So, you are going to call him to see what he can find out, right?"

"I suppose." I sighed. Though Ramirez had been helpful to us in the past, I didn't want to appear desperate for attention, either.

"Stop stressing. Ramirez totally likes you. He just needs to work through some issues. He'll come around, just continue to give him time, like you've been doing. You'll see." She looked fairly satisfied with herself, her pep-talk complete.

I wondered what had brought that on. "What? What is it you know?" I demanded, surprising her with my sharp tone.

She tried acting nonchalant, realizing she had said too much. "My TPD source might have provided me with a few juicy nuggets about our hottie detective." She shrugged, her tone non-committal.

"Spill," I gritted out, agitated she had been holding out on me.

"Whoa, Cujo." She groaned after taking in my expression.

"Still waiting…" I replied tersely.

"All right, all right." She put a hand up in surrender before continuing, "I wasn't going to say anything until I had a chance to do a bit more snooping, but now that you've asked me so nicely, I guess I can 'spill.' All I ask in return is that you abstain from shooting the messenger." It was my turn to groan, she was clearly enjoying this. What I had done to deserve such torture, I wasn't quite sure.

"You remember Serena Fenton, the gal we met the other night at Charlie's party?" she finally asked, chewing absently on a nail.

"Tall, leggy thing, weighs in at about 120? Perfect skin with even more perfect flowing locks? Basically, a dead ringer for Charlize Theron?"

She nodded and focused more intently on the poor nail before answering, "You forgot to mention the part about her being married to Congressman Fenton."

"Well," I mock-scoffed, "I thought that part was a given.

Yeah, clearly I remember meeting Serena Fenton. What about her?"

"She's Ramirez's ex," she replied dryly.

"She's whaaat?" Given the look I received, I realized I might have yelled a little too loudly. "He was married to her?"

"Not married, though I have it on good authority they were a couple for a number of years." I put my head in my hands. "If it makes you feel any better, she left Ramirez for Congressman Bob."

"Oh yeah, loads," I replied sarcastically.

"Of course, he wasn't a congressman back then, but there had been rumblings of political aspirations." She prattled on about his rise in the ranks, but I had stopped listening. Ramirez might no longer be on Serena's radar, she was most definitely still messing with his. "Anyway, rumor has it our young congressman's wife aspired to bigger and better stature, mansions, cars…things she would never get out of a relationship—"

"With a cop," I finished. And no, it didn't make me feel any better. "That's kinda shallow and a pretty awful thing to do to someone like Ramirez."

Leah nodded. "I hope it helps to explain a few things. It isn't about you, AJ," she paused. "Well actually, it is. My source said you were the first gal our boy has taken a shine to since Serena. His words, not mine."

"Wait a minute—how does your TPD source know so much about Ramirez's love life, anyway?"

"Giving away my trade secrets should cost you something," she teased, until I threw another threatening glance her way. "Ok, ok. He plays poker with him every Tuesday night."

Ah, the Tuesday night poker game. Huh. And here I thought guys just drank beer and smoked cigars. Who knew they talked about feelings too? Somehow, I highly doubted Ramirez went out of his way to share his with the group, though perhaps Leah's source was keeping tabs for other reasons, or other persons? I put that thought out of my head for the time-being. I had enough other stuff on my plate without my overactive imagination putting its big fat foot into it, too.

* * *

I waited until I knew Ramirez was on his dinner break to place the call. I was uncharacteristically nervous, though any conversation with the detective gave me butterflies, had me weak in the knees and all that other good stuff. These were, however, a different kind of nerves—ones derived from having knowledge I wasn't supposed to have. Even though the conversation I would be having with him had no bearing on his former love life, I felt as though I wore that knowledge like a "Hello, my name is Obvious" badge. He was a detective, and from my experience, a pretty darn good one.

I sighed as I scrolled through my phone's contact list, chuckling when I found his name. Leah had apparently commandeered my phone at some point and added a photo to Ramirez's contact info. Funny girl—her selection was Clint Eastwood as Dirty Harry. Laughing, I quickly moved to the letter "S" and sure enough, she had added photos for both Stanton brothers. For Abe —the brother I was sure had a crush on her—she had inserted her personal favorite, a photo of Tom Selleck as Magnum, P.I. and for Elijah, selected her second favorite detective, Matt Houston a la Lee Horsely. I had pegged him as a Mike Hammer type, but whatever. I bit the proverbial bullet and scrolled back to Dirty Harry.

Just my luck, Ramirez picked up on the first ring. His husky voice filled the connection, "AJ, to what do I owe the pleasure? Are you coming over to share my dinner with me? I made a couple of peanut butter and pickle sandwiches. Your favorite." I sighed, indeed it was.

I'd introduced Ramirez to my childhood vice a few months ago. Initially, he'd been disgusted by the odd coupling, but after a sizable amount of persuasion on my part, he gave in and after one glorious bite, called me a genius. In retrospect, he might have been referring to the sandwich. More importantly, the majority of his meals from that day forward consisted of two PB and pickle delights, though honestly, I wondered how he managed the second alone.

"Um, thanks, but I kind of had a long day and I need to get some stuff done here." I was totally flubbing it but if he noticed, he didn't make any mention, so I quickly filled him in on the events of the day.

He was silent for a moment before responding, "So, I take it you want me to talk to my TPD buddies about the investigation and see if anything can be done to speed the process along?"

"Well, I'm not sure about speeding the process along, but yeah, if you could see what you can find out, that would be helpful. It would mean a lot."

I knew my response sounded a bit canned. Darn it, the knowledge of his former relationship with Serena Fenton was making me act goofy. If he noticed my distraction, I was thankful he didn't press me for details. I certainly wasn't prepared to breech that subject. Someday maybe, or would I? I put myself in his shoes for a moment. What would Ramirez do?

He would wait, I decided. And because I cared about him, I would to do the same. It was settled—I would allow him to share the details of his past if and when he was ready. In the meantime, I'd just have to suck it up and get over this discomfort I was feeling. No sense making a mountain out of a mole hill, or whatever it was my dad used to say. I realized Ramirez had been talking during my pontification and had paused, either awaiting a response, or realizing I hadn't been paying attention.

Silly me, I decided to play it off with a stellar, "Um yeah, that would be great."

Ramirez chuckled. I imagined him on the other end, shaking his head, his eyes crinkling with amusement. "I was just saying dinner would be lonely without you, but that I would see what I could find out from TPD."

Something about the way he said it made me wonder about that second sandwich. Had he always packed it, in case I joined him? Nah, that couldn't be possible, could it? Perhaps Detective Jonah Ramirez wasn't such a mystery after all.

Maybe I hadn't been looking at the right clues.

CHAPTER SIX

A few days later…

It was a refreshingly cool spring day, so Nicoh and I elected to sit out in the covered backyard patio. As we nestled on one of the overstuffed outdoor wicker couches, Nicoh dozed, snoring quietly as his head rested carelessly on my thigh. I looked down at him, absently stroking his velvety ear—a bit envious of his ability to transition to a relaxed state. Physically, I felt as though I could be equally content, but mentally I was all over the place. I processed the events of the past few days—work, Charlie's party, Parker's sudden absence, the search and recovery of his body—even Leah's news about Ramirez's ex rattled around in my head.

I sighed. Nope, there was definitely no way I could join Nicoh in a nap, no matter how enticing I found the gentle rhythms of his breathing and paws drumming against the couch as he chased the elusive Pandora. I stifled a yawn, if I could be that…that…

I was so deep in thought I hadn't heard Ramirez calling my name. I looked up, squinting in the direction of his voice. His lips moved silently, his usually even gaze wild, as he repeated the same word over and over. I realized his arms were pinned with barbs and chains, shredding his clothing and piercing his tender skin. If he was in pain, he refused to allow me to witness his suffering. Instead, he continued to cast desperate glances at me… no…behind me. When I moved to assist him, he immediately shook his head from side to side. Suddenly, there was pressure against my throat, crushing my windpipe. I struggled for breath, the lack of oxygen making me fuzzy. As I lost focus, I caught a hazy glimpse of Ramirez struggling to free himself and realized I had been mistaken, he hadn't been uttering a word. It had been a name. Death.

I woke—my scream silent as I bolted upright, knocking Nicoh from my lap. He moaned sleepily, readjusting himself so that his head rested on a sofa cushion. Once comfortable, he emitted a guttural snore, oblivious to my ghastly dream. I wasn't sure how I'd managed to fall asleep and was glad the beep of my cell phone had woken me.

The afternoon had turned to night since we had ventured to the patio and the air drew a chill, forcing me to wrap my arms around myself as I pulled the phone from my pocket. I hadn't realized how warm Nicoh's head had been until his retreat to the other side of the couch. Sighing, I looked at phone's tiny screen, confused by the cryptic text message: *YOU CANT ESCAPE WHO YOU ARE ARIANNA*. Again, the number was unavailable. Taking everything else into consideration, this was getting just plain weird. Perhaps I would need to ask Ramirez for advice but seriously, who could it be? It was funny how the dreams were starting to coincide with the messages. I shrugged it off and shifted from the couch, being careful not to disturb the snoring beast again after the hard day he'd had.

As I shuffled inside, I wondered when Leah would be home and if she'd had any luck tracking down her TPD contact like she'd planned. As if her ears had been burning, my phone rang and sure enough, the ringtone was hers.

"I was just thinking about you, girl. Were your spidey senses working overtime, or what?" I paused before adding, "By the way, where the heck are you?" There was a lot of shuffling before she responded. Only it wasn't Leah.

Instead, a male voice chirped in my ear, "Arianna, it's been awhile." Given the crackly feedback, I recognized it as a recording. The voice was also vaguely familiar.

"Just wanted you to know, the time has come. You can't escape who, or what, you are." A quick laugh filled the connection before the recording ended and the call disconnected.

Though the words mirrored the text messages, what disturbed me even more was the caller's laugh. It's almost conversational quality caught me off-guard, forcing me back to a time when Leah had been kidnapped and nearly killed. It had been months earlier, but events were still clear in my mind, as was the voice of her captor—the same voice from the recording.

Winslow Clark.

Panic built as I struggled to rationalize the situation. I had been assured both Clark and his father, Theodore Winslow, were locked away in secured FBI facilities. It had to be a farce. He was under constant surveillance, in a psychiatric ward. How would he have gotten a hold of my best friend's cell number, or her phone, or her?

The exercise in rationalization clearly failing, I gritted my teeth and dialed Ramirez's number while several dozen thoughts, combined with a few colorful adjectives, ran through my mind. Impatiently, I counted the rings and contemplated leaving a voice-mail message when he answered.

Unlike our earlier conversation, his voice was clipped, "AJ, twice in one day."

Sensing he was in the middle of something important, I

quickly told him about the text messages and recorded call from Leah's number, saving my suspicions regarding the caller's identity for last.

When Ramirez responded, his voice was only a hint more congenial. "Why am I just now hearing about this?" Ok, perhaps the congenial tone had been wishful thinking on my part.

"Err…" Not my most profound, snappy response to date. "Well, at first I figured it was a joke and—"

"After that?" Ramirez demanded.

"After that, it just seemed silly…err…I guess…I guess I didn't want to seem needy."

Ramirez sighed. This time, his voice softened, "AJ, you are anything but needy. Sometimes I wish…I wish you needed me more. I'm sorry if I gave you that impression. Or made you feel like you couldn't come to me." He paused for a moment, his voice returning to its steely predecessor, "I'll see what I can find out about Clark and his father and at the very least, make sure they are where they're supposed to be. I'll also try to determine what permissions they've been granted for phone calls and visitors. In the meantime, contact Leah, though I'm sure she is fine. The caller probably cloned her phone. Err—hang on a second." There were muffled voices in the background before he placed me on mute.

He returned a few minutes later. "Sorry about that. One of the other detectives had some information, about Parker Harris. I'll share it with you, knowing you'll turn around and share it with Leah, but I'm warning you, if this ends up in the media, regardless of whether her name is associated with it…" He didn't finish the thought, leaving me to draw my own conclusions. If he'd been going for effect, it worked. I swore under my breath.

Apparently satisfied, Ramirez continued, "The Medical Examiner's Office has tentatively identified the body pulled from Tempe Town Lake as Parker Harris." I exhaled, Leah and I had been right. "Based upon the condition of the body, the ME confirmed he was dead before he went into the water."

"Wait, what do you mean 'condition of the body'?"

"Without getting too Patricia Cornwell on you, as you always say, Harris sustained significant internal injuries. Meaning there was no way he made it into the lake on his own—he was already dead."

"I don't understand," my voice came out as a croak. "Are you saying someone *dumped* Parker into the lake?"

"Someone not only dumped him into the lake, that person—or persons—may have also inflicted his injuries, or been present when they occurred."

"Someone…killed Parker…on purpose?" I stuttered. "As in foul play?" I certainly hadn't seen that puck coming down the pipe.

"Harris was definitely killed, then dumped. He didn't drown. Someone threw him in the lake, after the fact."

"But…but it could have…could have been an accident, right? Parker could have accidentally died and then…and then…" I struggled to make the pieces fit an alternative ending, "whoever found him…I don't know, freaked out and dumped his body… because they were afraid?"

"No, AJ. There were clear signs of a struggle—elsewhere. It's likely he was knocked out or somehow incapacitated to the point he could no longer defend himself, then killed. There was no accident about it. He was killed. Murdered." Ramirez paused but not nearly long enough for my mind to fully process it all.

"Harris was likely dumped in an attempt to mask the cause of death, by someone smart enough to realize the body would get tangled up, weighed down or at the very least, hidden from view. Of course, they also risked the possibility the lake would be dredged or drained but by that point, the body would have decomposed, making the cause of death difficult, if not impossible, to identify. Smart, but not smart enough to realize a storm was on the horizon. All the cunning in the world is no match for Mother Nature."

Again, voices murmured in the background on Ramirez's end. This time, however, he didn't mute the conversation and when he returned, something in his tone had changed.

"AJ, there's more," he sighed and was quiet for a moment, "TPD arrested one suspect and are questioning a second person of interest."

I groaned. I hated that phrase and Ramirez knew it. Weren't all people, in some respect, interesting?

Ramirez ignored me. "They've arrested Charlie Wilson—"

"What? That's ridiculous. Charlie might be the biggest pain in the you-know-what since Scrappy Doo joined Scooby and the gang, but he certainly wouldn't scuffle with anyone, much less kill them. What did they think his motive was—Parker's revolting fashion sense? And the murder weapon—a tube of overly-priced hair product?" I laughed, sounding a bit like a crazed circus clown after an hour with an audience filled with rambunctious five-year-olds.

"Not exactly..." Ramirez replied slowly, almost cautiously, "but there's still more." I rolled my eyes. Wasn't there always? "The person they are currently questioning...is Leah."

CHAPTER SEVEN

I was out the door before Ramirez could utter another syllable, spouting a few choice words that would have made my mother's toes curl in horror and was probably quite a sight as I marched into the Tempe Police Department, fists curled, hair flying, armed with an Alaskan Malamute.

The desk sergeant held up a hand in an attempt to cite some police regulation—something about animals not being allowed in government buildings unless being utilized in a service capacity —while I announced my intentions to find Leah and strode purposefully down the hallway. I got as far as the double doors leading who knew where before he gruffly grabbed my arm. Not liking the physicality of the gesture, Nicoh growled in warning and the sergeant's eyes widened in surprise. Before the situation escalated, I raised my hands in surrender. I'd be no help to Leah if I got locked up right alongside her. The officer nodded and released his steely grip. That was gonna leave a mark, I thought dryly, though admittedly, it was my own fault. I had acted in haste and apologized to the officer. Satisfied I was no longer in mortal danger, Nicoh grumbled before sitting on his haunches, carefully placing his large frame directly between us, just in case.

The officer shook his head, his face stern as he informed me had I bothered to listen, I would have been able to see Leah once the detectives were finished talking to her. *Oops...way to muck that up, AJ*, I muttered to myself, expecting to be escorted to the sidewalk. Instead, he pointed to a row of plastic chairs lining the wall before returning to his desk.

A few minutes later, another officer, this one in plain clothes, emerged from the double doors I had attempted and failed to breach. He was tall like Ramirez but had the build of a heavyweight boxer with a roadmap of scars on his face to match. Given his size, I hated to see the other guy. His black hair was cropped short, military-style, making his broad features even more distinctive. His eyes were as dark as his hair and though I was sure he could have put my evil eye to shame—according to Leah, mine was pretty darn good—his gaze was thoughtful as he gave us each the once-over. After a long moment, he nodded at the desk sergeant before ushering us through the doors and down a long, sterile hallway with a half a dozen windowless doors on either side. He wasn't much of a talker, so we moved silently until he stopped at the third door on the left. Nicoh let out a low rumble as we entered and after giving him a hard look, the officer finally broke his silence.

"You know, the dog isn't supposed to be in here, Ms. Jackson,"

"Please call me AJ. And yes, Officer, the err...desk sergeant out front indicated as much. I'm used to taking Nicoh everywhere and honestly, wasn't thinking clearly when I came here. I assure you he is well-behaved and will be no trouble." I shot Nicoh a look of warning but he ignored me, electing to sniff the corners of the room. Like I said, he's well-behaved.

The officer nodded, gesturing to the table and chairs positioned in the center of the room. "It's Detective—Detective Jeremiah Vargas. I thought you and your sidekick would be more comfortable in here while Leah is finishing up."

"Nicoh is hardly a sidekick," I huffed, though there was no real anger behind it. I was more curious about the detective's casual reference to my best friend and said as much.

Vargas chuckled at my pursed lips. "*Ms. Campbell* and I have worked together on several occasions, bridging the gap between the media and police relations, that sort of thing." He shrugged as though it was common knowledge. It was not. "I've also been assigned to the Harris case." Ah, so this was Leah's contact within the Tempe Police Department—the one who also played poker with Ramirez. Her being brought in for questioning would make for interesting shop talk next Tuesday night.

"Have you seen her? Is she ok? And, just for the record, you guys are out of your confounded minds if you think she had anything to do with Parker's death. I mean, no disrespect, but what were you thinking, hauling her in as a person of interest?" I finished my spouting with an emphatic use of finger quotes.

Vargas shook his head, barely able to refrain from erupting in laughter. It was, after all, a serious matter. "Ramirez said you were a spitfire."

I blushed at the mention of Ramirez, but wasn't about to be deterred. "You said she was being questioned, yet you are here. When can I see her?"

"To answer your questions, yes I have seen her and she is fine. And, for the record, we did not haul her in. She came in on her own accord, after I mentioned her name had come up during the investigation. Besides, she was present when the body was recovered from the lake. My partner is currently interviewing her and should be about finished, so if you don't mind hanging tight, I'll leave you two here and bring her back when we've wrapped things up. Are you good with that, AJ?"

"She's not a suspect then?"

Vargas shook his head. "If she is as forthcoming as she typically tends to be, then she'll be free to go as soon as the interview is finished."

"What about Charlie? There's no way he had anything to do with any of this either. Surely, you can see that?" This time, Vargas said nothing, so I changed tactics. "What about the murder weapon or whatever it was that was used to kill Parker before his body was dumped into Tempe Town Lake?"

His brow rose ever-so-slightly as I belatedly clamped my mouth shut. In true AJ form, I had said too much and probably gotten Ramirez into trouble in the process. Vargas' top lip twitched—I made a mental note to mention that to Ramirez, as it could be handy tip for poker night—but instead of pressing me, he departed, his tall frame barely dodging the door jamb as he passed.

I took the opportunity to look around the room. At first, it looked like any other conference room, but upon closer inspection I realized the table was bolted to the concrete floor. The walls, painted a lovely puce, were barren except for two opaque windows, which I could only assume were two-way mirrors. An interrogation room. Just great, AJ, now what have you gotten yourself into? Any more "sharing" and I'd end up in a cell with Charlie. Self-consciously, I glanced at the two-way and wondered if anyone was looking back. Detective Vargas thought we'd be more comfortable in here? Right.

Twenty minutes and several furtive glances at the mirror later, the door burst open and a blond blur flew in and nearly knocked me over, hugging me fiercely. Awkwardly, I attempted to stand and hug her back, but nearly dumped us both onto the floor in the process. Leah chuckled lightly as we broke our embrace.

I immediately noticed how tired and uncharacteristically pale she looked. Bags were visible under her bloodshot, red-rimmed eyes. From the way it stuck out in tangled clumps, it was apparent she had also been running her hands through her usually spiky hair—unless she'd stopped to run backward through a wind tunnel before making her way to the police station. Either way, I hoped she wouldn't catch her reflection in the two-way.

"You ok?" I asked, before making a slight gesture toward the mirrors.

She nodded. "I'm fine for now. Let's get out of here before they change their minds and I have to update my Facebook status from single to incarcerated."

I collected Nicoh, currently sporting an impressive bored look which, in case you weren't aware, involves sprawling on his side in an effort to take up as much real estate as possible, while emitting an equally large puddle of drool. The three of us made haste and retreated from the police station, waving briefly at the desk sergeant who grunted in return. Once we had cleared the threshold, I looked at Leah.

"What about Charlie? We can't just leave him here."

Leah shook her head and wearily replied, "They are still questioning him and from what I've heard, he's not going anywhere anytime soon."

"Maybe they'll at least allow visitors when they are done? I doubt he's faring well." I shuddered at the thought of Charlie Wilson, in jail.

"There's nothing we can do for him here. Let's just go home and I'll fill you in."

"Ok, I guess we'll meet you at home, then."

"Just one thing?" she asked as she unlocked the door to her SUV.

"Yeah?"

"Make some margaritas when you get there. Actually, you'd better make a pitcher."

* * *

Leah looked a bit better after a shower and a few applications of a good hair detangler. The tiredness that surrounded her eyes was still visible, but she beamed when she spied the snacks I had prepared: green chili salsa, guacamole, flour chips from Aunt Chilada's and of course, a pitcher of fresh-squeezed lime margaritas.

"Mmm," she crooned, stuffing a guacamole-laden chip into her mouth while I liberally poured the elixir into Ball jars I had frozen for such an occasion. "This hits the spot."

I took a healthy sip of my own beverage and nodded. "Good stuff."

"Indeed," was her only response as we munched in silence for several minutes.

"So," I put some distance between myself and the food, "I met your…friend, Detective Vargas."

"Jere?" Leah mumbled through a mouthful of chips and salsa. "Yeah, he's a good guy."

"Right….*Jere*. How come this is the first I'm hearing about him?"

She shrugged, pretending to analyze the flakiness of her chip. "There's nothing to tell. He's been a good source of info for me in the past and helped me run down a few details on occasion, while I've ensured nuggets were placed in the paper when needed. Stuff like that."

"Huh." I wasn't totally buying whatever she was attempting to sell, but had more pressing items on my mind. "So what happened? Why did they think you had information about Parker's murder?"

"I know, right? You can imagine my surprise when I showed up to ask Vargas some questions and he informs me I'm at the top of his list of people to question. Me!" She threw her hands up in exasperation.

"But why?" I asked, equally perplexed.

"Because they found an unidentified earring at the scene—meaning it wasn't attached to an ear at the time—and our pal Charlie was gracious enough to let the cops know he'd seen me wearing a pair just like them at his party," she huffed. "Anyway, *that* is how I came to be one of TPD's main persons of interest, after Charlie, of course."

"Wow, I hadn't even realized you'd lost an earring that night." I thought back to the party and our drive home.

"Crap, me either. They were cheap and pinching my ears, so I took them off and threw them in my bag. I never gave them another thought and until Vargas and his partner showed me the evidence bag, had no idea one had fallen out."

"Or made its way to the scene—which was where, by the way? Are we still talking about the area of the lake where Natalie found the tie and shoe, or where Parker was pulled out?"

"Neither, actually. As it turns out, Parker did *not* just accidentally fall into the lake after an evening of drinks at Charlie's party." Though Ramirez had relayed similar information, I shuddered as she blew out a deep breath. "The current theory is some altercation took place that either rendered Parker unconscious or incapacitated him to the point he was no longer a threat. Once he was out of commission…" She shook her head, unable to continue.

When she spoke again, her voice was barely a whisper, "It appears he took a series of blows to the mid-section, which damaged several vital organs and caused him to eventually bleed-out internally."

"They can't think Charlie would do that to Parker…to anyone…with his fists."

"Not his fists," she replied, her voice even quieter, "with his 1959 Cadillac Eldorado."

"Big Bess?" I screeched, causing Nicoh to howl. "They believe Charlie hit Parker—or ran over him—with his car?"

"Err, more like gouged him repeatedly, with her hurking tail-fins while Parker was pinned between the car and the wall." I gasped, mainly out of horror, but partially out of disgust. "Anyway, it appears it all went down in Charlie's parking garage, which is now considered the primary crime scene and lucky me, also where my earring was found."

I groaned, thrusting my face into my hands. This was worse than a bad remake of *Christine*. "This is just so awful. And I don't mean to seem juvenile, but gross. Please tell me they're sure Parker was unconscious?"

She shook her head. "Incapacitated for sure, but they don't know if he was completely unconscious when the impact occurred…if they ever will."

"Just awful," I murmured. I'd never been a fan of Parker's, but no one—not even Parker—deserved to die like that. "It would take someone pretty bent to concoct something sick like that. Charlie's a twerp, but he's not twisted. Struggling with Parker or even incapacitating him would be out of character, but to use Big Bess to *kill* him? No way. Charlie loves that car in an 'it's ok to love your car but don't loooove your car' sort of way." I shook my head.

If you happen to be knowledgeable about classic cars, you're likely familiar with the 1959 Eldorado. She's one big bad beast, all chrome and metal and definitive of an era long past. Not swank and trendy like Charlie's usual baubles. No, Big Bess was definitely not flashy enough to suit Charlie's usual needs.

Charlie liked his clothes, his penthouse, his possessions—even his daily driver, a sporty new Aston Martin something or other—but he *loved* Big Bess, probably as much as he loved himself. Don't ask me why. Charlie liked the latest and greatest toys but when it came to this car, for whatever reason, she broke his mold of perfection.

I'd often wondered if his beloved grandfather had once owned one, causing Charlie to lust after it as a means of emulating the famous man. I shrugged, whatever his rationale, once he'd found his Eldorado, he had to have her.

Big Bess—former name unknown—had been a California girl all her life, meaning she was free of the elements brought into play by harsher climates. She'd been owned by the widow of the man who had originally purchased her in 1959. Since that time, she'd only been driven 328 miles and spent the rest of her days in a climate-controlled garage—Big Bess, not the widow.

Charlie paid a lot of pretty pennies for her. The day she arrived in Arizona, Charlie had been uncharacteristically childlike and filled with pride. As they unloaded her from the transport, he'd carefully shammied her fin to fin, top to bottom. It was the only time I'd seen him show such emotion, which was how I knew Charlie would never risk damaging her, no matter how angry he was with Parker. Perhaps that sounds cruel—weighing the importance of a car over that of a human life—but that was Charlie.

"So did Big Bess show any signs of—"

"Damage?" Leah finished, which was probably a good thing, considering my mind had drifted toward something more gory, as in Parker goo. Yucko. "Neither a dent nor a scratch—that car is a tank. Besides, the killer wiped her down pretty well after he did the deed." I grimaced at Leah's choice of words, the margaritas were definitely kicking in. "But once the crime scene techs got done, they were able to find trace evidence."

"Trace, as in belonging to Parker?" I couldn't help but formulate a visual.

"Um, yeah…fabric, skin, blood…you know…trace."

"Well, thanks for that, Ms. CSI Tempe. I get what trace is, but can you honestly tell me they believe Charlie would actually risk A, ruining a perfectly good manicure by knocking Parker wonky; B, messing up a designer suit—no matter how white or ugly—and

C, destroying his beloved car? And, let's not forget, he'd still had to have the wherewithal to clean up after himself before dumping Parker in the lake?"

Leah looked at me evenly. "Not in a million years."

"Exactly, which is why this is so ridiculous. Even if you forget the bad stuff—like Parker being dead—and crawl into Charlie's world for a minute, there's no way he would risk having a bunch of sweaty crime lab techs man-handle his car."

"True, but for the record, I'm not sure he knows about that, so on the off-chance we talk to him in the near future, hold off on bringing it up. As it is, I hear he's not doing so hot."

I scoffed, "Not doing so hot? Of course he's not doing so hot. He's just been arrested. For murder."

"Well, I heard he's lost it a couple of times."

"Lost it, as in he had a tantrum?

"No, it was more like a mental break. From what I was told, he started acting out while riding in the back of the police car—complaining about hand sanitizer and the tragedy of faux leather."

"Uh, that's not exactly a mental break. That's Charlie."

She shook her head. "It wasn't just that. It quickly escalated to ranting and by the time they processed him, he was so incoherent, a specialist had to be brought in to confirm he didn't need to be hospitalized. The ranting eventually stopped, but he clammed up altogether."

"As you and I both know, Charlie's used to being the center of attention—good or bad—but he's typically also able to control the situation. Not so in this case." Leah nodded in agreement. "So, before he stopped talking, he obviously had no issue identifying your earring. How did you manage to talk your way out of that one, anyway?"

Leah laughed, but was not smiling as she did so. "Yeah, that. I just told them what I told you. I thought I had thrown them both into my purse at the party. At some point, one of them must have

fallen out and someone, maybe Parker's killer, picked it up and…
I don't know…used it as a diversion at the crime scene? Anyway,
several witnesses corroborated seeing us leave the party, so for the
time-being the earring is considered circumstantial evidence.
They may have more questions for me as the investigation
progresses, though," she shook her head in frustration.

"So don't leave town, the country, yada yada? Guess that
means the all-expenses-paid trip to Hawaii is out."

"Pretty much, though Vargas knows where to find me if he
needs me." She smirked. "As for Charlie, besides the earring bit,
they've gotten squat out of him."

"Typical Charlie, so frustrating. Doesn't he realize the longer
he holds out, the longer he's going to be sitting in a six by eight as
suspect numero uno?" I was thoroughly exasperated. "Surely his
lawyer can convince him it's in his best interest—as an innocent
party—to be as forthcoming as possible, as soon as possible?"

At the mention of a lawyer, Leah scrunched her nose. "Yeah,
about that—Charlie's refused counsel so far." I groaned, slapping
my forehead. She tapped her chin thoughtfully. "But I'm willing
to bet he'd chat with an old friend."

CHAPTER EIGHT

Through her contact at TPD, now known as Detective Jeremiah "Jere" Vargas, Leah was able to work her magic, enabling me to have a brief conversation with Charlie the following morning. Whether Charlie would see me or not was an entirely different story, one that I would tackle later. Leah'd had her fill of police hospitality and quickly opted-out of this excursion. Someone had to stay behind and keep the surly Alaskan Malamute company, she insisted, leaving me to wonder which of us had actually drawn the shorter straw.

When I arrived at the police station the next morning, Vargas was nowhere to be found, but had made arrangements with the desk sergeant on duty, a wiry woman in her late 40s with an iron handshake and expression that revealed nothing.

"Detective Vargas said you'd want to see Charlie Wilson," though she worked hard to mask it, her voice hinted at a slight accent, West Virginia, perhaps?

She gave me an appraising glance. "You do realize that Mr. Wilson has been arrested for murder?" The way she drew out the word "murder" indicated she thought I was too naive to know what I was getting myself into. She hesitated for a moment, expecting me to bolt after learning I'd made a wrong turn on the way to meet with my accountant.

I gritted my teeth. "Yes, I'm here to see my friend, Charlie Wilson."

The sergeant sniffed at my curt response but said nothing as she made a quick phone called in a muttered tone. Once done, she looked at me squarely, her jaw set and stance rigid.

"Very well, then. One of the detectives will be up to collect you momentarily."

Despite being dismissed with a nod in the direction of my favorite plastic chairs, I elected to remain standing. Call it my stubborn side. Sensing the sergeant's eyes burning into the back of my head, I turned to level my own glare. She immediately averted her steely gaze and internally, I reveled in the small win. That was until I realized her focus had actually been directed toward a sturdy-looking officer emerging from the hallway. I was glad I'd held out on that victory dance.

"Ms. Jackson? I'm Detective Sanchez," his voice boomed but was friendly as he extended a beefy hand. I returned the gesture and took the opportunity to marvel at his sausage-like fingers as they clasped mine, thankful I hadn't brought Nicoh, who would have been salivating while looking around for deli mustard. Eww. The handshake itself—once you got over its resemblance to meat —was surprisingly soft, yet firm. Nothing like the death grip the desk sergeant had wielded.

"Mr. Wilson has agreed to see you, but before I take you over to the other building to see him, I'd like to cover a few of our ground rules. I see you managed to leave your canine at home this time around, which is a good start."

I blew out a long breath. Apparently, I was making quite a name for myself around here. Not good. Sanchez took in my expression and chuckled, outlining the visitor protocol as we exited one building and entered the adjacent, presumably the jail. If he was curious about my visit, he made no indication.

"Are you one of the investigating officers on Parker Harris' case?" I was careful not to reference Charlie or murder in the same sentence. Sanchez nodded but did not elaborate. "So, you really think you've got enough evidence to move forward?" I prompted.

Sanchez was a little less friendly this time around. "Charlie Wilson wouldn't be sitting in that cell if we didn't, Ms. Jackson."

Thankfully, we had arrived at our destination: a small room, about half the size of the one in the other building. Like the other, it was devoid of sunlight or windows and armored with two-way mirrors. The fluorescent lighting was severe, making the drab interior look even more putrid. A worn steel table was positioned in the center of the room, with picnic style benches on either side. All were bolted to the floor in a not so picnic-like way. Someone had graced the top of the table with several slurs I will not repeat. Let's just say that during childhood, my mouth had its share of run-ins with Borax. A few of the more colorful phrases even made me blush, which is saying a lot, given my familiarity with the powdered soap.

Sanchez seemed amused by my discomfort and pointed to one of the benches, etched with drawings that mirrored the sentiments on the tabletop. I pretended to ignore them and sat, hoping to position myself in a way that would allow privacy from the mirrors, but the setup of the room prevented me from doing so. I glanced around and scowled, realizing Sanchez had slipped out. After a few minutes he returned, with Charlie in tow.

It was as bad as I had expected. Charlie's once-pressed chinos were crinkled and dingy with dirt and grime. His button-down shirt was not tucked and showed significant signs of perspiration; his usual handmade Italian leather shoes replaced with canvas slip-ons. Except for the obvious wear and tear, I would have sworn he was channeling his inner *Miami Vice*. Charlie himself told a less Don Johnson-like story. His typically gelled locks hung limply, covering his eyes and trailing down his cheekbones, now flanked with shadows. His pouty lips formed a thin line as he plunked onto the bench opposite of mine, not appearing to care where the mirrors were positioned. He'd obviously spent a great deal of time in this room.

"Well, at least you got to keep the digs. You know how orange washes you out and tends to make you look…chunky," I attempted to lighten the mood and obvious humiliation Charlie was feeling.

His lips formed a tiny smile. "For now, it seems. Though, it is kind of ironic I'd be allergic to prison couture."

"Huh. I didn't know a doctor's note would work in this situation. That's good to know."

This time, the laugh reached his eyes. "You know me well, AJ, better than most."

Sanchez cleared his throat, reminding us of his presence. "You have thirty minutes. I suggest you make the most of them," he turned to leave, glancing back as he reached the door, "and yes, Ms. Jackson, I'll be watching."

Charlie spoke once Sanchez made his exit, "In case you were wondering, I didn't do it." He eyed me slowly, gauging my reaction.

"Which part of 'it' are you referencing?" I crossed my arms and stared at him evenly.

Charlie blanched, clearly expecting me to take him at his word. Perhaps a part of me did, but I wasn't a complete dolt. Before I gave him the confirmation he needed, he owed me some darn good answers.

After a long moment, he nodded. "First, I didn't have a physical altercation with Parker on that night, or any night. Regardless of what you think about my character, I don't believe in violence as a resolution, no matter the problem. Second, I did not lure him to the parking garage under any circumstances, much less to render him unconscious, as indicated by my first point. Third, I would not and did not impale him with the fins of my car. Fourth, I did not have anything to do with dumping him into Tempe Town Lake. And last, I do not know, nor did I conspire with the individual or individuals who did." He snarled out the last bit, perhaps not only for my benefit but for that of Detective Sanchez and any other law enforcement type lurking behind the mirror. After brushing hair from his eyes, he snarkily added, in true Charlie form, "It's not my style."

"Um, yeah, I got that," I replied in a low tone, my lips barely moving, "but given your current situation, how can you so easily dismiss the fact your best friend was brutally murdered and then dumped like he was nothing more than yesterday's trash? Especially considering you are now suspect numero uno?" The last part came out in a growl and I was sure to our friends behind the glass, I sounded a little crazed. I didn't care. My message was for one person. "Don't be such a nitwit, Charlie! Wake up and smell the Starbucks!"

Given his raised brow and sour expression, Charlie had heard me loud and clear. For once, he wouldn't be able to throw a tantrum or bully his way out, not when someone had orchestrated the situation so beautifully he'd come out looking like the perfect primary suspect.

Charlie finally conceded, "I agree. My attitude has been a bit…vexatious, given the circumstances. But I want to impress upon you, I do take the situation seriously." In an uncharacteristic, self-conscious gesture, he ran his hands through his hair. "Perhaps initially…my ego…did not allow me to fully comprehend the ramifications. But after giving it some thought, I've realized a few things about myself. I guess what I'm trying to tell you, is while I had nothing to do with Parker's death directly, there are things from the past—decisions I made, actions I could have taken but didn't—that were just as damaging."

"I'm not sure I'm completely following you."

Charlie nodded, leaning his forearms on his thighs. "As you know, Parker and I went way back, along with Greg. All of us had privileged upbringings and were from well-respected families, so it was natural for us to hang out in high school, head off to Harvard together and things like that. We had access to anything and everything, which made us arrogant. Given our money, status and combined inherent business acumen—as we used to like to think of it—we thought we were a force to be reckoned with. What we didn't take into account was our individual egos. We were in a constant state of one-upping the other and even that was never enough.

"Until recently, I hadn't considered Greg wasn't like Parker. Or me. Not really. He was a good friend. A loyal friend, and far more trusting than Parker and I deserved. We'd take risks—and I mean *huge* risks—and there would be Greg, trying to rationalize things, trying to reason with us, doing anything he could think of to get us to come down off our high horses.

"Looking back, I think we actually enjoyed torturing him with all our elaborate plans and schemes, sometimes literally bullying him into joining our fun. For a long time, things typically worked out in our favor, so we'd tease him mercilessly about his cautiousness. Then came the times things didn't go our way. Still, Parker and I played with money like we'd printed it ourselves.

"I won't go into all the boring details, but for years making money off other people's investments was child's play to us. They made money. We made money. Everybody was happy. Then, a few years ago, Parker took things a step further. Both Greg and I had reservations about complicating our money-making formula, but by that point Parker's ego was even more inflated than my own.

"He'd resort to sneaking around behind our backs if it suited him. Our formula didn't require too many rules, but that one was a deal-breaker. Undaunted, he took unnecessary risks, often based upon a whim or whatever interested him at that moment. In his mind, it was a shortcut to the formula and had the potential for yielding bigger gains. More often than not, however, his off-formula risks resulted in disaster.

"During one of Parker's whims, he dabbled with a large amount of money Greg had earmarked from a group of investors setting up a foundation to fund several local hospices and critical care treatment facilities. All were privately-funded, relying on external sources—like the investment group—for the livelihood of their programs and services, as well as for future research and development. The market unexpectedly turned south and thanks to Parker, the money Greg had raised was gone, leaving nothing for the facilities and no returns for the investors. Parker was off to his next venture while Greg scrambled to recoup the money. Though he salvaged what he could—even using his own money—many of the facilities were either forced to limit services or eliminate others. And, of course, there was the blowback from the investors themselves. Greg was devastated, though Parker had been the one to facilitate the deed. As a group, it wasn't one of our finest moments," Charlie paused to catch his breath.

I realized I could have taken that moment to absolve him by telling him it would all be ok, but I refused to lie to him, or to myself. In truth, I was angry. Seething, actually. And though I fought to keep my face a blank slate, it took everything in me not to turn my back on him and walk out of that room and his life. It was either that or punch him in the throat. I preferred the latter, followed by the prior, and was giving it some serious thought when Charlie interjected.

"That wasn't even the worst part. Parker laughed when he

found out. Laughed. He figured if anything, it would teach Greg to keep his money to himself and not waste it on charity cases."

"What did *you* do?" I managed to grit out, surprising Charlie.

"That's the point, isn't it? I didn't *do* anything." He focused on his hands, as though eye contact with me would be too painful. "I did nothing to stop Parker. And nothing to help Greg."

Something finally clicked into place. "That's why Greg killed himself, isn't it?" Charlie's silence only accelerated my growing fury.

"He's dead because of your stupid…games, your insurmountable egos and your inability to show some spine. You allowed your friend—one of your best friends—to suffer, alone." Charlie flinched at the harshness of my reprimand, but I wasn't in the mood to be merciful.

"Greg couldn't deal with the guilt. And still, you did nothing to ease his pain. No kind words. No show of support. Nothing. He felt he had no other way out. That's it, isn't it?" By this point, my fingernails were digging into my palms. I refused to look at Charlie, fearful I would punch him after all. In the end, I decided a swift sock to the throat was better than he deserved.

As if reading my mind, Charlie spoke, his voice barely a whisper, "So you think I deserve this." It was not a question and for a long while, I did not give him the benefit of a response.

I was still seething when I finally did speak, but my blood had cooled to a somewhat more rational level, "You know what they say about karma, Charlie. So yes, in some ways, you made your own bed. You are a crappy friend and an even worse judge of character. I do not, however, think you deserve to be set up for Parker's murder, any more than I think he deserved to be killed and dumped like garbage. He was an awful, despicable human being, but that doesn't give someone the right to be judge, jury and executioner. No human gets that hook. By putting his blood on their hands, they've only succeeded in taking on his burden themselves. Killing Parker didn't right a wrong. It just created two wrongs."

Charlie nodded, whether he agreed I wasn't sure, though I hoped he'd taken some of what I'd said to heart. I certainly wasn't going to ease up on him, but I needed to change the direction of the conversation, as time was ticking away,

"So, what caused you and Parker to be at odds during the White Party?" I shrugged when he raised his eyebrows. "I saw the daggers you were shooting at him, not to mention your body language. Anyone who knows you even a smidgen realized something was off between the two of you."

"I wasn't aware I was being that obvious." He sighed as he picked invisible fuzz from his trousers. "Parker had done it again. He'd been taking liberties with funds that weren't his, hedging bets, losing millions. As before, Parker took no responsibility, nor could he be bothered with the consequences incurred by others."

"Oh no," I groaned, "who was affected this time, more investors with privately-funded recipients?"

Charlie shook his head. "It's not something I'm willing to discuss yet. I'm sure there will be rumblings in the media before long, though I'm hoping there will be a resolution for the absentee funds and perhaps even another backer." I tried pressing him but he simply raised a hand before continuing, "Like I said, if it's meant to come out, it will soon enough. No offense, but I don't need your best friend pushing things along."

"Really, Charlie?" My temper flared at his insinuation, especially when Leah wasn't present to defend herself. "So it's ok to have a crack reporter at your disposal when it's convenient, when it benefits you directly, but when it comes to something that actually matters to someone else—"

"No, AJ, that is not what I meant," he gritted out, his own emotions rising. "It's just…better for the parties involved to keep things under wraps for the time-being. Got it?"

I shook my head. I did not understand, nor did I buy it. With Charlie, it was never that simple. He was withholding pertinent details, for reasons other than the ones he was intent on convincing me of. Why was that?

It was clear he wasn't going to budge on the subject, so I shifted the conversation, "So, based upon what you've told me, Parker could have had a sizable list of haters. Anyone you like for president of that club?"

"No, Detective Jackson, I couldn't even begin to narrow down that list." I didn't appreciate his sarcasm but managed to keep a snarky retort from escaping. "And murder?" He shook his head. "I don't see anyone, no matter what list they're on, going to that extreme."

"Desperate times breed desperate measures, Charlie."

"True statement, but I'd hardly fit into that category."

"And yet, here you sit."

"Harsh, AJ, harsh. But again, true," he conceded. "Still, I can't believe someone would be spiteful enough to kill him, much less go to the effort of framing me while doing it." Charlie appeared surprised, if not miffed. Clearly, it hadn't occurred to him he might be considered as unseemly of a character as Parker had been. Given the current situation and his new accommodations, I decided it wasn't the best time to rub salt in the wound.

"So, do you have an alibi?"

Charlie frowned, shaking his head from side to side. He studied the two-way before responding, his tone low, "Not one that can be validated. Unfortunately, the security cameras show me exiting the building shortly before Parker was attacked."

"What about the cameras inside the parking garage?"

"They weren't on."

"Isn't that a bit of a coincidence?"

Charlie's pressed his lips together in a tight line. "Not really."

"Seriously, *that's* all you've got?" My voice raised an octave.

I hadn't meant it to, but we were talking about murder charges. Argh, sometimes I wanted to strangle him myself.

"It wasn't a coincidence because I was the one who took them offline."

I groaned and knocked my head against the table. The icy steel of its structure did nothing to tamper the burn of frustration. "Charlie Wilson. Why. Would. You. Do. That? What were you thinking? Weren't you concerned about the lack of security?"

He shrugged. "I own the building, so I can do whatever I want, whenever I want." As if that was an acceptable answer. I popped my head up and gave him my best evil eye, letting him know as much.

"I was making some…adjustments in the parking garage I didn't want to have recorded. I wasn't finished by the time the party started, so I left the cameras off."

I couldn't read his expression, but my gut told me that he was lying, again. Charlie didn't make adjustments to anything himself, he had people for that. So what would have been so important he'd needed to turn those cameras off?

"Big Bess needed to be fixed?" I tossed out.

The question threw him. "Huh?"

"The adjustments you were making in the parking garage, they were on Big Bess?"

"Oh, yeah, um, new door locks." New door locks? Riiight. Now Charlie was a mechanic?

"Interesting." Charlie noted my sarcastic response, but continued to scrutinize the invisible fuzz on his pants. "So, where did you go after the party? Did anyone see you?"

He blew out a deep breath, still refusing to make eye contact. "I decided the clean up could wait until later, so I let you, Leah, Arch, the caterers and the rest of the staff leave. Basically, I just wanted to get some fresh air. I had a few cocktails at the party after seeing Parker, so I went for a walk to clear my mind. I did so on occasion but honestly, not that often.

"After the party, I found myself heading down to the lake, toward the walking path. It was quiet, given the hour, which provided me the solace I sought. Of course, it was also dark out so in the areas where the pathway was unlit, I tripped probably a half a dozen times." He chuckled to himself. "It was my own fault for asking the bartender for such a liberal pour. Anyway, despite the darkness—and my clumsiness—I kept walking, until I'd lost all track of time. It's funny, at the time I was pleased I never crossed paths with another person. Now, not so much."

I muffled a curse, but noting the amused look Charlie was giving me, realized I had not been successful in keeping the sailor to myself. My Borax days long over, I made a mental note to run to Costco. If this conversation was any indication, it looked like I'd soon need a generous supply.

"Which direction did you walk along the lake?"

"Um, east toward Scottsdale Road. Like I said, I don't walk the pathway very often. I prefer Tempe Beach Park or just going to the gym."

Of course he did. Charlie had dedicated an entire floor in his building to a state-of-the-art workout room for himself and the other residents. And yet, he'd chosen that night to go for a walk along the lake—in the direction and roughly around the time Parker had been dumped—possibly even passed the same location where his body had been recovered.

He had also conveniently disarmed the security cameras that would have captured the events in the parking garage that night— cameras that would have eliminated him as a suspect and identified Parker's killer in the process. One thing was for sure, Charlie had worked himself into a real cluster, if not the perfect setup.

"I heard they towed my car to their facility." He nodded toward the two-way as I pursed my lips. Leave it to Charlie to be concerned about possessions at a time like this. "Do you think they will at least attempt to be careful with her?"

Honestly, I didn't know.

"They are professionals, not a bunch of hooligans hauling her off to their seedy chop shop. Short answer is yes, I think the police will do what is necessary to retrieve the evidence they need in a respectful and cautious manner." It was the best response I could offer him given the circumstances. For whatever it was worth, Charlie seemed to appreciate that.

Looking at my watch, I realized our time was nearly up. I mentally kicked myself for not getting more from Charlie, though there were some details he'd purposely kept close to the vest. Some pretty important ones, I feared. As if reading my mind, the door opened and Detective Sanchez's massive presence filled its frame.

"Time's up, Wilson. Hope you two had a nice chat."

I smirked. He would know.

I turned to Charlie, disappointed any last minute questions had eluded me and noticed he'd carefully tucked his emotions away as he returned to his stiff, unreadable demeanor that resembled a figure in the House of Wax. Perhaps this was how Charlie survived the world of the six foot by eight foot cell, by letting his thoughts and feelings slide away. I wondered if Human Charlie would return on my next visit, or if he would even make it that long.

As Sanchez and another officer led him out, Charlie paused briefly. "I appreciate you coming, AJ. When the chips finally fall, it's good to know who your friends are and who'll be there to help you pick up the pieces." A flicker of Human Charlie flashed in his eyes, gone just as quickly as he disappeared through the doorway. I felt a pang of sadness, mixed with curiosity. Were we indeed, friends?

Sanchez returned a moment later. "He's right, you know. You

are a good friend. Doesn't seem a guy like Wilson would have many, so you can imagine my surprise when not one, but two of you showed up."

"What?" I blinked. "Two of us? Leah hasn't seen Charlie yet."

"Not Ms. Campbell. Natalie Ingram, the deceased's girlfriend." You could have blown me over. "She was here yesterday and insisted on being the first to see him after we were done with him." He shook his head. "It's an interesting dynamic those two have."

Sanchez didn't elaborate, leaving me to wonder why Charlie hadn't mentioned it. I thought about our conversation, having to drag crumbs out of him and the odd shifts in personality. Had Charlie fed me the details I'd wanted? Or the ones he wanted me to believe? Had the new, more humane Charlie been real, or simply created for my benefit?

Perhaps I had never known Charlie Wilson at all.

CHAPTER NINE

As they shuffled him back to his luxury suite, he realized he was fortunate to have friends like AJ. He was also painfully aware he hadn't always been the greatest friend in return. Heck, who was he kidding? He'd never been a decent friend, much less a good one. Did he even know how? People who were kind and selfless like AJ and Leah seemed to and still they befriended him, even given his shortcomings in that department. He hadn't ever taken others into consideration. People were disposable commodities who lived and breathed to cater to his needs, not beings with feelings, thoughts and needs of their own. No, he'd never been a true friend. AJ was more of one than he deserved.

He plopped onto the threadbare cot—one that probably had never seen better days—and was rewarded with creaky springs that irritatingly jabbed him in the backside. He sighed, it was another reminder he was not a guest but a ward of his accommodations.

The first reality check emerged as he was unceremoniously collected from his penthouse, stuffed into the back of an ancient and extremely pungent smelling police cruiser and escorted to the station. As they rode in stuffy, unairconditioned silence, beads of sweat quickly turned to drips, stinging his eyes as they continued their journey over his cheeks and onto the thighs of his Armani slacks. Given their smug profiles, the detectives appeared to be enjoying his growing discomfort.

Charlie sniffed, crinkling his nose as he tried to identify the source of the stench permeating the cracked, well-used interior—a cross between a men's locker room and the dance clubs Parker liked to frequent in Scottsdale. He managed to refrain from cringing as he continued to examine his surroundings, which were devoid of any personalization. The only extravagance he observed was the hot pink air fresheners—some hideous floral combo—that failed miserably at keeping the odors at bay. Though the cruiser had been recently vacuumed, as evident by the lines in the plucky-looking carpet and was free from trash or debris, he could see the dirt and grime—*wait, was that mold?*—and some other gunk infesting the crevices of the seats and window sills. Best not to touch anything more than necessary, and even those body parts might need a Brillo later. To date, it had been the longest ten minutes of his life. He hoped it wouldn't be the first of many.

Back in his cell, Charlie shuddered at the memory. The irony was not lost on him. The car ride had been just that—the first of many of the longest minutes of his existence. He was disgusted by his own vanity—that the fear of others knowing he'd been arrested superseded that of what the police thought he'd done. Well, his selfishness had certainly caught up with him two-fold, hadn't it?

It was the reason he'd spent the better part of the day marveling at the fact people like AJ existed. They were so different from him and from Parker. They actually cared when he was in trouble or hurting. He wondered if he would have done the same had the situation been reversed, and shrugged, already knowing the answer. It was a futile, senseless exercise.

Still, AJ had come. It didn't matter if she believed in his innocence. Or did it? He surprised himself—yes, it did. It definitely mattered what AJ thought. After digesting their conversation, he realized he hadn't done much to help himself in that arena. Still, she'd left knowing he was innocent…of killing Parker, at least. As for his complicity in other matters—he was no fool—he'd seen the judgment in her eyes, no matter how hard she'd fought to mask it. She was only human, after all.

Again, he chuckled briefly at the irony, becoming somber as he reflected on how poorly he'd treated her over the years. No matter how decent and generous she had been, he'd taken and never asked what he could do in return. She'd stuck around because of who and how she was. He felt something odd when he was around her, other than the annoyance she spurned in him—admiration, perhaps? She was a determined soul, with insurmountable resolve and loyalty…fierce loyalty. For a moment, he felt something new. Shame. He had desperately wanted to break down and ask her for help.

He put his head in his sweating palms when it hit him—AJ was already helping him, whether she realized it or not.

* * *

I arrived home, feeling no better than I'd left though admittedly, no worse, either. I'd gotten the opportunity to visit with Charlie, which had been my intention—only now, I had far more questions than answers. It had been surprising to learn to Natalie had not only gone to see him at the jail, but insisted on being the first in line to do so. Had she been there to deem his innocence? Or guilt?

I was mulling things over when Leah entered the kitchen, carrying a jar of chunky peanut butter in one hand and a bag of plain M&M's in the other, with Nicoh in close pursuit. One glance at his nose told me that she'd been sharing her snack with him, but it was Leah's wide-eyed expression that confirmed it.

Apparently, my BFF had been so engrossed in snackapaloosa, she hadn't heard me enter the house. Feeding a large canine can be so distracting and noisy. Realizing she was busted, she gave up trying to hide the evidence, instead making an animated show of screwing the lid back on the half-empty jar.

"You seriously didn't—" I pointed at the bag she had placed on the counter.

"I'm not a complete dunce. Of course I didn't feed him the M&M's," she scoffed, noticing my gaze had moved to the peanut butter, "and no, I did not allow him to eat directly out of the jar. I put a smidge on his nose to stop the howling. I swear my ears were starting to bleed."

"Well, I'm happy to know I won't need to run out and purchase a people-only jar, aside from the one we already reserve for people who double-dip or allow crumbs to get mixed in, that is."

"Eww, I hate that," Leah replied.

"Totally gross. So, did the peanut butter on the nose trick actually work?"

"Yup, Nicoh was so busy lapping at it, he forgot his reason for being noisy in the first place."

"You mean nosy, don't you?" As expected, our abrupt laughter caused Nicoh to resume his howling.

"How'd the visit with Charlie go?" she asked after we managed to get him calmed back down, though no further peanut butter was traumatized in the process.

"It was interesting, to say the least." I filled her in on our conversation and how Sanchez revealed I hadn't been Charlie's only visitor.

"Wow, Natalie must have connections or something. Charlie was tied up—quite literally—until you and I left yesterday. She must have someone on the inside keeping her up to date."

"Someone like Vargas, wouldn't you say?"

"Maybe…" Absently, I reached into the bag of M&M's while Leah proceeded to pluck the brown ones out. When she placed them on the counter, I tilted my head in Nicoh's direction, noting the saliva dripping in anticipation as he focused on the movement of our hands. And of course, the unattended M&M's. Leah sighed and scooped the stray morsels back into the bag, while Nicoh grumbled.

"It wasn't Vargas, though. I'm pretty sure he's never met Natalie."

"Oh?" I raised my eyebrows.

"Argh, get your mind out of the M&M's bag. Just so you know, it came up when I asked him about the guests who'd attended Charlie's White Party—whether any of them had any prior run-ins with the law. The answer was no, other than a few drunk and disorderlies, no assault, battery—"

"Or murder."

"Not one of them."

"So, what do you make of Natalie visiting Charlie then?"

"Not sure. Like you said, maybe she needed her own confirmation whether Charlie could have killed Parker. Prior to that, I would have guessed the thought wouldn't have occurred to her, especially not after the way she glommed onto him at the lake."

I nodded my head. "That was odd. Even Charlie appeared to think so. You remember the look on his face? Certainly didn't seem like they had much interaction before that. In fact, the only thing they had in common was Parker. Well, and Greg, I guess."

"I wonder if she knew about their business challenges. You would think if she had, she would've made a point of staying as far away from the two of them—especially Parker—as she could."

"Yeah, but you know what they say—keep your friends close…" I didn't need to finish that thought—there was only way to know for sure—we had to go to the source.

* * *

After a quick phone call, we learned Natalie was volunteering at one of the long term care facilities near Old Town Scottsdale that afternoon. She eagerly agreed to meet us at Los Olivos after her shift, a nearby family-owned Mexican restaurant and one of our local favorites. In addition to being a well-known historical land-mark, they had the most delicious fresh-squeezed lime margaritas this side of the border. Don't get me wrong—Leah and I weren't trying to get the goods out of Natalie by plying her with alcohol, we simply figured a refreshing beverage couldn't hurt.

Just to be sure, we tested the pitcher Manuel had graciously brought out as we munched on chips, salsa and hot sauce while waiting in the outdoor patio area. As if on cue, our snacking prompted Nicoh to moan like a belligerent moose as he show-cased his displeasure for the other diners. We received several understanding nods, since many of them were also accompanied by their canine companions. Thankfully, Natalie arrived before he started in on the full-blown howling, forcing them to change their minds.

"Hey ladies!" She placed a supersized Hermes bag on a seat of its own before carefully sitting in the chair next to it. I handed her a margarita, which she drained in one noisy gulp.

"Delicious!" she exclaimed, pushing her glass forward for a refill. Leah complied and gave me a quick glance, neither of us sure whether we should be impressed, or frightened.

Noting our bewildered expressions, Natalie blushed. "Sorry… rough day. We lost one of our residents today. Chalk it up to being emotionally drained." She studied the ice cubes in her margarita while pushing the lime around with her thumb.

"We are truly sorry, Natalie," Leah replied, while I nodded. "Your day must have been long all around—I'm sure you've heard about Charlie, too?"

"Yeah, I visited him at the jail. It was awful." She shuddered. "I don't care what the police think they have on him, there's no way he killed Parker, or had anything to do with the whole messy incident." Messy incident? That was an interesting way to phrase it, like Charlie had been accused of spilling red wine on Parker's white suit. Natalie inhaled before taking another large swig of margarita. At this rate, we'd need to get her a separate pitcher.

I made a mental note to grab her car keys before pressing her on her last comment. "You seem pretty sure about Charlie's innocence."

Natalie wagged her finger at me and snickered. "Pah-leeze! It's totally not Charlie's style, nor would it have occurred to him. Now Parker, on the other hand, wouldn't have hesitated to eliminate anyone or anything in his way." She drained her glass and shakily reached for the pitcher. It slid precariously close to the edge of the table and would have made its way onto the ground had I not managed to catch it. Rather than putting it back, I nonchalantly scooted it to the opposite side of the table and made a show of moving the chips and salsa into its place, hoping it would encourage her to eat a few.

While I maneuvered bowls, Leah kept the conversation moving forward, "What do you think Charlie and Parker were having a row about the night of the White Party?"

I stifled a snort. That was Leah for you—no sense beating around the bush when you can just cut it down. And, another reason I was the photographer and she was the reporter—I did all my work behind the scenes while she preferred being front and center and in your face. She was darn good at it too. Like pit bull good.

An indescribable expression passed over Natalie's pert face as she smoothed her immaculate pantsuit with one hand, gripping the margarita glass with the other. "Oh, you know how those two were. I'm sure Parker had his mitts on something Charlie wanted."

"Is that what Charlie told you?" I kept my tone even, careful not to push her.

"Charlie didn't tell me squat. Parker either"—she giggled —"before he died, of course." She nervously clinked her ice cubes.

Before Natalie requested another refill, Leah distracted her, "So this had nothing to with the money Parker lost?"

I glanced at her. Risky, Leah, very risky. She raised a finger behind the table to let me know she knew what she was doing. It certainly ignited something. Natalie's death grip turned to white knuckles as anger flared, but vanished as she carefully tucked it away with the rest of her emotions.

"I wouldn't know anything about that," she replied flatly, still obsessed with torturing those poor ice cubes. "It was between Charlie and Parker—only Charlie and Parker. Parker never shared the specifics of his business dealings with me and I never asked. Our relationship worked best that way."

It sounded like a relationship of convenience more than one of love or respect. Not that it surprised me, anything more would have been inconvenient for Parker. No wonder Natalie seemed all over the charts when it came to coping with her boyfriend's death.

She changed the subject before we could ask her additional questions about their relationship. "On a cheerier note, I was able to raise enough money this past month to add new rehabilitation and counseling services at a few of the facilities."

As Natalie prattled on, we listened with interest. It was truly inspiring to hear about the work she was doing. I noticed the more engrossed we were, the more she animated she became. Clearly, she was proud of what she'd accomplished and loved to receive praise. I seriously doubted Parker had provided her with much positive reinforcement, which explained why she so eagerly ate up any attention she was given.

Speaking of eating, both Leah and I noticed how little she'd had, given the amount of liquor she'd imbibed. It was curious, I hadn't seen her drink any more while we talked, but somehow she'd managed to put away almost another entire pitcher. A solid liquid diet wasn't great for anyone, especially not a tiny little thing like Natalie. I was about to suggest some other appetizer or food options but she glanced at her watch and suddenly launched out of her seat.

"Oh, I've gotta jet. I have plans this evening."

Quickly thanking us, she collected her massive handbag—which made her look like a six-year-old after raiding her mother's closet—blew a few air kisses and started to leave when I called after her, "Hey, Nat—why don't you hold up for a sec? We'll pay our tab and share a taxi with you."

She waved a hand at me. "Thanks, but I've already got a ride. You didn't actually think I'd risk ending up like Parker, did you?" She giggled, giving us a quick wink as she departed.

Once she was at a safe distance, Leah slid from her seat and ventured after our tipsy friend. She returned moments later, frowning.

"What?"

"Well, Natalie's designated driver picked her up." An odd expression crossed her face. "Driving a blue Audi R8." Parker's car.

"One more thing—the driver was female." I gave her a long look. Parker had no female relatives. In fact, there wasn't anyone who should have been driving his car. Leah nodded in return, having come to the same conclusion. I looked longingly at the empty margarita pitcher. Like Alice, down the rabbit hole we would go.

CHAPTER TEN

Leah hadn't seen more than a wisp of the driver's auburn hair as Natalie hopped into the Audi and the two hightailed it out of there. Fortunately, they hadn't caught her lurking either. She'd been careful to press herself against the building, hiding in the shadows as she attempted to spy on them. Compliments of her reporter's repertoire, I guessed.

Natalie had been hanging out at Parker's house when we'd previously seen her. Neither of us was sure whether she'd continued taking up residence there once his body had been recovered. What perplexed us was—other than Charlie and Natalie—Parker really had no other friends or immediate family. So who would have taken possession of his car so soon?

Manuel stopped by our table, an equally curious look spanning his face. "The margaritas were not to your liking?" Leah and I exchanged glances after looking at the empty pitcher in front of us.

"Manuel, what would give you that impression?" I asked, rocking it back and forth.

He shook his head and pointed to a large plastic cup, the type found at any convenience store, leaning against one of the table legs. In it was a watered-down version of the limey goodness from our previously full pitcher.

"Err, our friend had a hole in her glass?" Leah offered as the confused server picked up the cup and peered at the contents.

Hole in her facade was more like it. I wasn't sure whether I should have been relieved to learn Natalie wasn't a lush, or annoyed because she'd played us for ninnies. For Manuel's purposes, however, we simply shrugged and added a few extra dollars to the tab, hoping he would chalk it up to a bunch of silly girls letting off steam after work. He narrowed his gaze, but seemed appeased and thanked us for our patronage, though didn't mention looking forward to seeing us next time, as was typically his custom.

As he retreated, Leah grumbled under her breath, "Great, now he thinks we're either drunk or a bunch of Fruity Pebbles."

"After that carefully scripted act, why do you think she risked leaving the cup?"

"Who knows, but it does mean that Natalie fed us those details…on purpose."

"Girl's good—I'll give her that."

"Indeed. I never even saw her hand leave the table, much less realize she was spinning a tale even taller than Krystle's and Alexis' shoulder pads."

Rolling my eyes at her campy *Dynasty* reference, I tapped my chin. "Does make you wonder, doesn't it—with what other forms of deception is our girl-next-door acquainted?"

"Oh, come on, AJ. Faking drunk is a far cry from *Impale and Dump Your Boyfriend: A Modern Girl's Guide to Giving a Jerk the Literal Heave-Ho.*" I winced at her choice of words, glad we were standing on the sidewalk waiting for our cab, safely out of Manuel's earshot.

"That's not what I'm saying. I think Natalie wanted to give us selective information with regards to Parker and Charlie. I have no idea why she felt the need to concoct such a farce. Maybe she felt guilty talking negatively about Parker?"

"I guess. You notice how she hasn't talked about him—I mean *really* talked about him—the way a girlfriend would? Not since that day at the lake, anyway. I don't know, it seems weird considering they'd been in a relationship for more than a couple of years."

"Maybe things had cooled down. Or, maybe it was just a relationship of convenience all along and it's her way of dealing with his death. We didn't spend much time with her after Parker was found. Maybe she's been going through all the phases of grief and we just haven't seen it."

"That's a lot of maybes," Leah commented. "One thing is for sure."

She had me intrigued. "What's that?"

She inhaled a deep breath. "The only way Charlie's getting out of this mess is if you and I figure out who killed Parker."

* * *

We contemplated the situation in silence on the cab ride home while Nicoh nestled between us—yes, there are pet-friendly cabs —his head on my lap and tail in Leah's, oblivious to the drama unfolding. Knowing Leah, she had already devised some sort of scheme in that devilish brain of hers. Before I had a chance to press her for details, my phone rang. Ramirez.

"AJ, I've got some news about Winslow Clark." I hadn't been expecting that but quickly told him I was putting him on speaker-phone so Leah could join us. "I talked to some friends at the FBI, who talked to their contacts, who in turn confirmed Clark and his father, Theodore Winslow, are in two separate, secured facilities. Both are in single-occupant cells for twenty-three hours a day— with one for exercise—under armed guard. Neither has had outside contact, other than with their court-appointed counsel, which they've both denounced. No incoming or outgoing mail. No visitors. No calls. Nothing. Time essentially stopped for them the minute they stepped into federal custody, meaning—"

"Neither was directly responsible for the messages," Leah finished.

"That is correct."

"Couldn't they have minions on the outside doing their dirty work, ones they were in contact with before they were captured and incarcerated?" she asked.

"Minions?" Despite the gravity of the conversation, I had to stifle a snort when I heard the confusion in Ramirez's voice.

"Yeah, minions. Haven't you heard of *Despicable Me*?" Leah asked, incredulous.

"Despicable…what? What are you talking about?" Ramirez's tone grew terse so I gestured for Leah to zip it, for all the good it did.

"Minions, Detective, as in flunkies, followers, groupies, cohorts—"

"Point taken, Leah," I growled.

"She does have a point." Ramirez added. "Just because Clark and his father claimed to have worked off the grid for all those years doesn't mean they did so alone. They could have built up a small following, a group of people to be their eyes and ears whenever and wherever they were needed."

"Sounds risky," I commented, "especially considering how paranoid and arrogant those two are. I'm not sure they'd trust just anyone with their dirty work."

"True enough," Ramirez replied, "but you'd be surprised what kind of people are out there on the fringe. Clark and Winslow may have found themselves a few true believers. Either one of them could easily incite a loyal following. Anyway, I've got another friend looking into the source of your messages. He may not be able to extract much, but for everyone's sanity it's worth a shot."

"Another FBI friend?"

"Let's just say a friend with connections."

I looked at Leah and shrugged. "So, in the meantime, is there anything you need us to do?"

"Just go about things as you normally would. The important thing is to not change your behavior, meaning don't purposely engage him. Don't reply to the texts. Let the voicemails run their course and forward whatever you get to me. Hopefully by tomorrow, we'll have more on him than we have today."

Leah scrunched her face. "I don't know, Detective. That advice sounds more reactive than proactive. Considering you and your friend are making AJ here a guinea pig, I'm not sure I like it." I voiced a similar opinion.

"Gals, please. Do not do anything rash. Let my guy look into it. If something comes up, you'll be the first to know. For once, please do what I ask." It was the non-detective part of him that was asking.

"Well, Leah, he did say please," I let out an exaggerated sigh for his benefit as we grinned at one another.

"You two," Ramirez growled.

Leah smirked at the phone. "Now that we've gotten Clark out of the way, we have a few interesting items of our own to share. AJ, why don't you tell the detective about your conversation with Charlie?"

I stared, unaware we'd decided to share, but had no recourse other than to shake my head, collect my thoughts and give Ramirez a quick rundown of the visit. Once finished, Leah jumped in and started telling him about cocktail hour with Natalie. I threw my hands up, beyond exasperation. She made no bones about laughing at me as she gave Ramirez a play-by-play of Natalie's bizarre behavior while masking her alcohol consumption.

After several moments of deafening silence, Ramirez spoke, "I know the way the two of you think, especially when you have your minds set on something. I can't begin to emphasize this enough—do not get involved in your own investigation—let TPD do their job. I'm warning you, if you interfere, I'll arrest you both myself.

"Besides, you're off-base about Natalie Ingram. She's got an iron-clad alibi and that's all I'm going to say about that. So leave it alone," he sighed into the phone. "I've got to get back to it. Stay out of trouble, both of you."

Even before we'd heard the connection break, we had no intention of following Ramirez's advice. Instead, we plotted the next steps of Operation Charlie. Sure, it was amateur hour and we knew it, but we also knew the cops had enough evidence to convince the County Attorney to lock Charlie away for the rest of his life, or worse.

Leah scribbled furiously on her trusty notepad. "We should see if we can get a look at the security videos from Charlie's building," she mumbled absently to herself, nibbling on a non-existent nail. She glanced up to catch me looking at her. "What?"

"Nothing," I replied, smiling warmly. "I'm just glad I have my partner-in-crime working with me on this."

"You know, I'm gonna remind you of that when Ramirez tosses us in lockup," she teased.

"Duly noted. Looking at the security footage is a good plan, provided TPD hasn't already confiscated all of it."

"Well, we know who to ask." Though dreading the conversation, we'd reluctantly agreed to have a chat with Arch. At the very least, we hoped he'd give us access to the information we needed. He was also on the list of partygoers, so we were technically killing two birds with one stone. Err, poor choice of words.

Anyway, considering Arch held more than a couple of the puzzle pieces we needed, a little visit to Charlie's assistant went straight to the top of our list.

Whether the world was ready for us or not, Operation Charlie was now underway.

* * *

Rather than calling ahead the next morning—no sense giving Arch an opportunity to escape—we checked in with Charlie's doorman, Stuart Klein.

Stu was a jovial guy, with a sharp wit and watchful eyes, cultivated from the years spent as an armored truck driver and security guard. He took his post at Charlie's building no less seriously. He was sweet and funny and knew how to make a girl blush, but if push came to shove, he wasn't someone you'd want to underestimate. He knew every trick in the book and could lay someone out flat before the devious thought had fully formed in their mind. I had often wondered how Charlie had managed to lure such a seasoned and loyal man.

Though Stu was several years Charlie's senior, he always referred to him as Mr. Wilson out of respect, whether Charlie deserved it or not. He was courteous to us as well and more than eager to watch Nicoh before Charlie allowed pets in the building. With more and more of his residents requiring companion-friendly accommodations, however, Charlie was forced to lift the ban, though his penthouse suite had been the final holdout. To this day, Nicoh was one of the few four-legged creatures to have graced the top floor, a feat that was five years in the making.

During that time, Stu and Nicoh developed quite a relationship. On the days I worked with Charlie—who knows why he needed a freelance photographer on call—Stu would share his lunch with Nicoh and tell him stories of the good old days, as though he was with his drinking buddies. Perhaps Stu took the opportunity to embellish a bit, whereas his human pals kept him in check. Either way, they were always excited to see one another, with Nicoh on his hind legs while Stu embraced him like a bear. It was endearing and a sight to see, considering Nicoh towered over the man by several inches. If Stu minded the dog slob Nicoh graced the top of his head with on each visit, he never complained.

Today was no different. Once reunited with his pal, Stu greeted us with a big smile. "Ms. Arianna, Ms. Leah, it's so nice to see you both, as always." He straightened his suit jacket and tie, tugging his cuffs down. "Terrible business about Mr. Wilson, just terrible."

"Actually, Stu, it's the reason we're here." Leah wagged her eyebrows at him conspiratorially. "We're planning on having a little…chat with Arch, to see if he remembers anything out of the ordinary the night of the White Party. And, since we're here, maybe we could ask you some questions, too?" It was always a plus to have a crack reporter on your team.

Stu nodded thoughtfully. "Mr. Wilson doesn't have many friends like you, that's for sure. If I can do something to help, then by all means, ask away. It's the least I can do."

"So you don't think he had any involvement in the murder, then?" Leah asked.

Stu gave her a sly look. "We both know Mr. Wilson, Ms. Leah, which means we both know he isn't capable of murder—not even the murder of someone as unscrupulous as Parker Harris. No, I doubt something as bawdy as cold-blooded murder would have entered his mind. Mr. Harris, on the other hand"—Stu sniffed in distaste—"would have been more amenable to something along those lines. Sorry, it's not respectful to speak ill of the dead." Leah and I nodded our understanding, though it wasn't the first time since Charlie had been arrested someone had made that observation about Parker's character.

"As for that night, I did see Mr. Harris and Ms. Ingram leave, both very alive and extremely tipsy, but neither of them returned. In fact, the only odd thing that occurred all evening was when Mr. Wilson stopped by my desk to say he was going out, but had misplaced his key card and indicated he would need me to buzz him back in.

"Like the other guests, he was a bit intoxicated so I offered to call him a taxi. He waved me off, saying he needed the fresh air and wanted to stretch his legs. As you know, he's not one for small talk nor does he go out of his way to be friendly, so I was surprised when he made a point of thanking me for my concern. In all the years I've worked for him, he's never thanked me once, so I was surprised by his sudden congeniality. In looking back, he seemed off his game—distracted, worried even."

"But not angry?" Leah prompted.

"Agitated maybe, but not angry—he rarely shows that kind of emotion. Tantrums…yes, but raging anger…no." We both nodded, quite familiar with Charlie's outbursts, which were more theatrical in nature than malicious or driven by heated emotion.

"What was he wearing when he left?" I asked.

Stu tapped his chin and chuckled. "He was wearing a white monkey suit—atrocious if you ask me—and a bit too retro for my taste." The suit both he and Parker had been wearing had indeed been retro, but it was a style that was back en vogue and both had likely known it. Whether they had planned on being triplets—with Arch in the mix—was still up in the air. Knowing Parker and Charlie, I thought not. In fact, I wouldn't have been surprised if Charlie's stylist had lost her job that night.

Stu continued. "Anyway, when I saw him, he was a bit more relaxed than usual. Shirt opened at the neck, but still very immaculate." I thought back to the only other time I had recently seen

Charlie so relaxed. It had been the morning of the party. He had been distracted then too. Something occurred to me.

"You said the neck of the shirt was open. Was he still wearing the tie?" Leah nodded, understanding the direction I was headed.

It took him longer to respond this time, "Yes, now that you mention it, he did have a tie on, hanging loose around his collar. Other than that, he looked like he was still in party mode, all the way down to his white shoes." He reached over and scratched Nicoh behind the ears.

"Was he carrying anything—like a wallet or keys?" Leah asked.

"Not that I could see, though his hands were in his trouser pockets most of the time. Of course, if he was going for a walk, I'd doubt he'd need car keys." Good point.

"Did he ever go to the garage this way?"

"No, he typically went directly from his elevator to the parking garage, so I rarely saw him." Stu squinted. "Ah, I see where you are going with this. You are trying to determine whether Mr. Wilson was attempting to create an alibi for himself the night of the party. That would be clever—very clever indeed."

Stu was right, but if we'd come to that conclusion, the police had likely done the same. Meaning, Leah and I would need to prove it hadn't been intentional—something forced Charlie off his game, causing him to be distracted, as Stu had indicated.

"What was Charlie like when he returned?" I asked.

Stuart shrugged. "He seemed the same."

"What about his clothes? Were they dirty? Disheveled in any way?"

"No, though it did seem like he had been running his hands through his hair. I know it always looks like that—you kids and your styles—but it was messier than usual." Again, I flashed back to the morning before the party, when Charlie had absently, and uncharacteristically, rubbed his hands through his hair.

"And his clothes?" Leah prompted.

"Except for the fact he wasn't wearing shoes or socks when he returned, there wasn't a spot on him."

"He was barefoot?" both Leah and I chimed at the same time, startling Stu.

"Sorry," Leah patted the man on the arm, we had been a bit shrill in our response. "You're saying he came back carrying his shoes?"

"No, he was barefoot all right, but his didn't have the shoes with him."

"Did you ask him about it?"

"I thought it was curious at the time, but it certainly wasn't my place to question him." He was right. Charlie wouldn't have taken kindly to being interrogated by his staff.

"Was he still wearing the tie?"

"That, I'm not sure about. The video should be able to confirm it one way or the other, though."

We nodded and turned our questioning back to Parker, though Stu had nothing out of the ordinary to report and his account of Parker's arrival and departure were the same as we'd previously heard. Natalie arrived early, waited for Parker and they went up to the penthouse together. What had happened to Parker once he'd left Natalie later that evening was anyone's guess.

"Did you talk to Natalie while she waited for Parker?" Leah asked.

"Yes, just small talk, mostly about her work. Turns out she volunteers at one of the hospitals where my wife works as respiratory therapist. Ms. Ingram knew my wife. Sweet girl, that one."

"Did she seem fidgety at all, or impatient? It was our understanding she and Parker chose to drive separately because she'd expected to be the one running late that evening."

Stu shook his head. "No, she didn't seem either. Said Mr. Harris had some last minute business meeting or something or other. Other than that, there's not much more to tell. Mr. Harris showed up and they took the elevator up to the penthouse. He was never very friendly." Stu scrunched his nose, clearly not a fan of the late Parker Harris. We nodded sympathetically. Parker hadn't been particularly cordial to anyone.

"And when they left?"

"Like I mentioned, lit but not wasted. I overheard Parker calling her a cab. She didn't seem totally thrilled about it. Not about the cab, but that he wasn't taking it with her. She was worried he might try to drive himself home. I overheard him say he wouldn't but she didn't seem convinced. I didn't actually see the cab arrive—it would've taken me too far away from my post —though I assumed she's taken it home and he…well, I guess we won't ever know." I glanced at Leah—that was one point we disagreed with Stu on—*someone* knew.

She swiftly changed the subject, "We understand there are several cameras positioned around the building."

Stu nodded. "Normally, I wouldn't share this type of information with anyone other than the police and that's only if they supply a warrant, but seeing how they've managed to get this whole thing backwards, I think Mr. Wilson would approve. Especially considering you're the only two who seem to care what happens to him and are interested in doing some real investigating."

"Thank you, Stu, though I'll be honest with you. I'm not sure what we're doing could technically be construed as 'investigating,' in anyone's book," I replied somberly.

Stu chuckled, waving off my comment. "Nonetheless, you're trying to do something positive for Mr. Wilson, which makes you the good guys…err, gals, in my book. Anyway, the cameras are currently placed here at the entrance, at the entrance to the elevator and throughout the parking garage."

"Charlie told me about the ones he recently installed in the penthouse," Leah added.

"Yup, he did that at my suggestion, right after he mentioned bringing his assistant back on. You know, for good measure." He winked but his expression was serious.

"You don't trust Arch?" I asked.

"It's not so much about trust as it is about putting Mr. Wilson's interests first. Now if you're asking me if I would personally trust the kid, the answer is no. Don't get me wrong, he appears harmless, but he's way too shifty for my liking. Typically, that doesn't mean anything by itself, but sometimes you just know to keep your eyes peeled when something feels hinky. You know what I mean?" We nodded that we did. "Anyway, if it had been me, I wouldn't have hired him back. Period. Now this happens and he's installed himself in the penthouse, doing who knows what. It doesn't sit right with me."

"Uh, you mean he's *living* in the penthouse?" Leah managed to ask as she did an Oscar-worthy job of masking her shock.

"Yup, he moved himself in the day the police took Mr. Wilson and hasn't been out since. My relief, Maynard, confirmed it."

I wondered what the heck Arch had been doing up there all this time. And more importantly, did Charlie know? "Wait…can't you see what he's up there doing using the cameras Charlie just installed?"

Stu shook his head. "Mr. Wilson wanted sole access to the penthouse's footage. Oh, his tech guy has access, too, but I don't know who *he* is. In fact, Mr. Wilson, the techie and I are probably the only ones, other than the two of you, who know about those cameras." Meaning TPD still hadn't gotten access to them, much less were even aware they existed.

Argh, had I known that, I would have asked Charlie when I'd seen him. Perhaps Leah and I could convince him to let someone —preferably us—monitor that feed in his absence? Certainly, he'd be able to see it was in his best interest once he learned Arch had been camping out in his penthouse, right? For now, all we could hope for was the next best thing.

"Stu, any chance we could have copies made of the footage you do have access to?" I asked.

"Sure, I can get you dups of the videos TPD took. No matter what people think of him, Mr. Wilson has always been doggedly thorough, and had the foresight to have second and third copies made and stored offsite. I'll make arrangements to have them brought over while you two are up chatting with Arch."

"You are truly a sweetheart, Stu. If you weren't already taken…" Leah gushed.

"Now, now, Ms. Leah, don't you let my wife hear you say that," the doorman teased. "She may just let you have me."

CHAPTER ELEVEN

Stu warned us Arch had access to the building's security feed, so we weren't surprised to find him waiting as we stepped off the elevator and into Charlie's penthouse. He'd probably been watching us from the comfort of his laptop all along. I hoped there was no audio, otherwise we were in for a short conversation. It did, however, make me wonder how secret the cameras *inside* the penthouse were—if Leah had found out about them, perhaps Arch had too? I fought the urge to look around but the instant he turned away, both Leah and I were craning our necks in awkward angles. Arch scowled when he swung back to face us, clearly inconvenienced by our intrusion.

"Why are you here?" His upper lip twitched, a cross between a smirk and a snarl. Billy Idol he was not.

Annoyed by his attitude, I quickly stepped toward him, closing the distance between us. The movement caught Arch off-guard and he staggered back a step as I continued to invade his space.

"Is that a rhetorical question, Arch?" My voice came out like sweet tea, thick and sugary, borderline diabetic. "Or are you just pretending to be a complete dolt? Because I'm pretty sure you already know the answer."

Leah and Nicoh had closed ranks and we faced him, three abreast, a united front. Or, more accurately, two cranky chicks and one ravenous canine, the latter of which was currently looking at Arch's legs like they were the last chicken wings on Earth. Temporarily subdued, Arch bowed his head in resignation.

"Now that we're all on the same page, we've just got one question for you. Are you going to help us get Charlie out of this mess, or what?" I crooked my eyebrow at him, a hint of malice in my tone.

After a moment, Arch sighed and to show his concession, shuffled to the open living room and motioned for us to sit. Leah nodded at me, but kept her poker face intact. We were both aware giving Arch any leeway would be a mistake. If we wanted compliance, we needed to maintain control of the situation, which in this case meant keeping the tension high.

Arch slumped into a modern, uncomfortable looking chair as far away from us as the space permitted. We selected our own seats and once settled, noticed he'd been keeping the penthouse tidy in Charlie's absence, just the way his boss would have liked it. The only addition to the stark decor was an enormous bouquet of vibrant purple orchids, artfully composed in a striking crystal vase.

Arch caught me admiring the display and elaborated, "I thought they might add a splash of color, improve the vibe… given all the negativity that's transpired the past few days." I nodded though I wasn't sure who, other than Arch, would have been around to enjoy them.

We sat for a few moments in awkward silence until Arch spoke. "In case you were wondering, I don't think Charlie killed Parker." Arch's statement may have effectively sliced through the tension, but it was his resolve that surprised me the most. "I don't have any proof and I'm betting neither of you do either. But we all know Charlie…and well, he couldn't have done it."

Pausing to survey our reactions, he exhaled deeply before continuing, "What I do know is Charlie let me go the night of the party immediately after the last guest left. He said the clean up could wait until later." He shrugged. "I was surprised. It was so unlike him to put things off. It had been a long day though, so I wasn't about to question him. As I got onto the elevator, he asked me to be in at my usual time. I didn't think anything more of it until he was arrested."

"What do you know about Charlie and Parker's relationship over the past few months?" Leah asked him casually.

"I assume you, like everyone else, noticed something was brewing between them at the White Party. I figured it had to be business-related, though recently it seemed like Charlie was trying to distance himself from Parker."

"Distance, such as…" I prompted.

"Charlie called Parker less, routinely ignored Parker's calls, even Parker himself. He avoided going to places and events where Parker would be and even went as far as having me tell Parker he wasn't here when he'd stop by. Stuff like that." He tapped his chin. "He did, however, talk to Natalie on occasion, even though he suspected Parker had put her up to it."

Leah snorted. "Parker had his girlfriend keeping tabs on Charlie? That's rich."

"Does seem pretty desperate, especially for Parker," I added, before turning to Arch. "When was the last time Parker came to see Charlie?"

"Hmm, it had to have been at least a couple of weeks before the party."

"And Charlie turned him away?"

"Actually, no. On that day, he agreed to see Parker. They went into the atrium and ten minutes later, Parker came back out, ignored me and left. Of course, that was nothing new. Parker always treated me like crap."

"Other than ignoring you, how did he appear as he was leaving?" I asked. "And how about Charlie, what was he like?"

"Hard to say with Parker, he was always annoyed about something. That day was no different. But like I said, he didn't speak to me. He wasn't bursting with joy, that's for sure." Arch shrugged. "Charlie was definitely more moody than usual after Parker's visit, but didn't say a word about it. Instead, he mumbled something about an errand and left. He didn't return by the time I had wrapped up for the day and when I arrived the following morning, he was back to his normal self. I'm sure you know what Charlie's 'normal' is like." He gave us a small, sad smile.

Honestly, I couldn't imagine working for Charlie full-time, much less as his assistant. Still, it was hard to sympathize with Arch, who was clearly reaping more from the situation than he was letting on. Mirroring my own thoughts, Leah rolled her eyes before changing the subject.

"What happened to the clothes Charlie wore the night of the White Party?"

"Err, I don't know. I assumed they went to the cleaners, as they normally did."

"You didn't handle that for Charlie?" I asked, genuinely curious. I certainly hadn't meant to imply anything and was surprised when Arch's eyes narrowed, letting a glimpse of his usual haughty attitude slip though.

"No, I did not *handle* Charlie's laundry. He had...has a service for that." He gritted through his teeth, barely managing to keep the snarkiness at bay.

Honestly, I hadn't intended to strike a nerve and had bigger fish to fry, so I quickly played it off. "Oh, right. Was it a scheduled laundry service?"

"Yeah, they came every day. I typically checked them in, collected the delivered items and handed the new ones off." Arch's feathers started to smooth and his talons were now safely retracted, though I had to bite my lip to keep from pointing out point that he actually did handle his boss' laundry.

Leah noted my amusement and intercepted, "So they came the day after the party to collect the previous day's clothes, which included the suit Charlie wore to the party?"

"I guess so, but they must have come early that day or maybe I was busy doing something else, because I never saw them."

"Did you ask Charlie about it?" Leah asked.

"No, by that time it was too late and everything happened so fast. All of sudden there were police everywhere. Then Charlie was arrested." He shook his head. "It was a nightmare. I forgot all about the laundry service after that, until you asked me just now. You think there's something there?"

"I doubt it," Leah replied. "We just wanted to cover our bases." We had bases? I raised an eyebrow at her and she shrugged in response, giving me a head nod to proceed.

"Who has access to the penthouse, and by access, I mean key cards, key codes or whatever it is you use?"

Arch nodded at my question. "It's a short list. Charlie, the doormen and I have key cards to the penthouse. Essentially, each resident has a set specifically for his or her condo, which also works at the building's exits and entrances. In addition to the key cards, each resident also has a unique key code to access the parking garage."

"So, you have a key code for the garage, too?" Leah asked.

"Me? No…why would I need a key code?"

"So you can park your car?"

"Oh," Arch laughed stiffly, "I don't own a car. I take the light rail to and from work."

"What do you do when Charlie needs you to run errands?" I excused myself to use the restroom, while Leah quickly added, "Oh sorry, I forgot. You don't do errands." I barely managed to contain my snickering.

"We have a car service if Charlie has tasks offsite." His tone indicated the question was bordering on the ridiculous. For once, I had to agree with him—she was actually trying to buy me some snoop time.

I peered into Charlie's room and found it to be as neat and orderly as it always was. No dust puppies here. As Arch prattled on, I moved down the hall and snuck a peek into the guest room and hit paydirt.

From all appearances, he had made himself quite comfortable in Charlie's absence and from the look of things, wasn't overly concerned with impromptu visits from Charlie's friends. Closets overflowed with clothes, while the bathroom countertop held dozens of hair care products and other miscellaneous toiletries. One thing was for sure, someone planned on staying for more than a few days. The rest of the room was as well-kept as the remainder of the penthouse. I quickly stepped into the hallway bathroom, ran the water and slipped back into the living room before my absence was noticed. If Arch suspected anything as I returned to my seat, he concealed it extremely well.

"Have you had any visitors since Charlie was arrested?"

"Other than Natalie and then Charlie's ex, the lawyer, the answer is no," He made no bones about repeatedly checking his watch. "I wouldn't have expected too many people. I don't mean to be rude…"

"Our apologies Arch, you've obviously got things to do, we'll let you get back to it." We'd probably gotten about as much out of him as we were going to. Besides, the details he hadn't elected to share were far more interesting.

"If we have any more questions, we'll know where to find you, won't we?" Leah laughed, but given the way Arch narrowed his eyes, I seriously doubted he found her amusing.

"Anyway, we'd best be going, Leah." I looked at her pointedly, before turning to Arch. "Thanks for your time. We appreciate it and I'm sure Charlie will too." He said nothing but followed us as I hauled Leah into the elevator, with Nicoh close on our heels. For once, my Alaskan Malamute was being more compliant than my BFF—go figure.

I gave Arch a finger wave, praying the doors would shut but Leah managed to get the last word in after all, "We'll let Charlie know you said hello." Arch's mouth tightened and as the elevator slid shut, he graced her with a long, hard look.

Apparently Arch wasn't the only one sporting a thistle in his paw. Nicoh huffed as we exited and made a beeline toward Stu's station, to the awaiting treats. Stu chuckled and after rewarding the grumbling beast—for what I had no clue—he provided us with DVDs of the security camera footage as promised. We waited until we were back at the car and safely tucked inside to discuss our conversation with Arch.

"Well, that went off without a hitch," Leah snarked.

"At least we didn't walk away empty-handed," I replied, a bit giddy about the discovery during my scouting mission. "Let's just say Arch has been taking full advantage of his boss' absence." I proceeded to share my observation of the guest room.

"Interesting…" she commented once I'd finished. "Do you think Charlie knows?"

"Are you kidding? I don't think Charlie would let his own mother stay, if she was still alive."

"Well, other than taking up residence, Arch wasn't much use for anything else," she grumbled.

I smirked. "On the contrary, my friend, not if you think about it in terms of what he didn't say."

"Ah, well, he never asked us a single question about Charlie."

"Exactly."

"Certainly a curious curiosity, if Nero Wolfe's Archie Goodwin ever had one."

A curious curiosity, indeed, no matter who was having it.

CHAPTER TWELVE

Leah and I were trying to determine out next move—watch the security camera videos or talk to Charlie, Natalie and the party attendees. Our decision was conveniently made for us with a single phone call. My chest tightened as my cell phone rang, registering another unavailable number. I cursed under my breath before answering, my voice sounding unusually sharp. Leah shot me a concerned look as I shook my head.

After a long moment of silence and another few where I stopped breathing, a familiar but somewhat grainy voice filled the other end of the connection, "AJ?"

I resumed breathing—it was definitely not my mystery texter or caller.

"Charlie, is that you?"

His reply was crackly, "I…I don't know how much time I have to talk. Can you come and see me?"

"Absolutely. In fact, Leah and I just left your penthouse and have some…things to discuss with you, too."

"Oh, ok…good, good. Yeah, please come…and bring her, too." The connection went dead.

The police station was only minutes away from Charlie's

building and upon entering for the third time, yet another desk sergeant greeted us, informing us we were on the list. I wondered if that was a good thing—given our recent track record, probably not.

"An officer will be up to collect you shortly. In the meantime, you will need to leave your canine with me."

After checking out the artillery strapped to his side, I wasn't about to dispute the issue. Instead, I patted Nicoh on the head and handed his lead to the sergeant. Nicoh was still miffed about the stint with Arch in Charlie's penthouse and happily complied with what he saw as a new source for potential snacks. As if on cue, the sergeant scruffed Nicoh under the chin and pulled a treat from a container behind his desk.

"You know," I commented dryly, "if you encourage him, you'll have to deal with him."

The sergeant laughed, a low rumble. "No worries. I've got three retired police dogs at home—all German Shepherds—I know the drill." I nodded, noticing how unusually quiet Leah suddenly was. I followed her gaze. Our police escort had arrived —Detective Jere Vargas. I smirked, this would be interesting.

"AJ…Leah…" the big man drawled, his eyes never leaving Leah, who was studying grout patterns on the floor. "You two ready to meet with Wilson?"

I nodded and gestured for him to lead the way. As we moved down the hallway, I noticed a spark of electricity in the air as Leah looked up at the detective shyly. Leah…shy? I stared at my friend, who had resorted to shuffling her Chuck Taylor's like a three-year-old as we moved into the conference room. It was arranged like the others with a simple set of table and chairs and of course, the two-way mirrors.

Fortunately, there was no time for embarrassing small talk, as a guard ushered Charlie in, a meaty hand clamped securely around his bicep. I barely contained a gasp. Charlie's appearance had changed dramatically in the hours since I had last seen him. This time, he was dressed in the jail-issued attire: an orange and white striped jumpsuit with canvas slippers. The ensemble was completed with wrist and leg irons, something I had not been prepared for. His hair, long devoid of styling products, hung limply as pieces strayed across his eyes while others danced beyond the tip of his nose. His usually tanned skin had a grayish cast, which under the fluorescent lights gave him a sallow, vitamin-deprived appearance. As he lifted his chin, I noticed his lips were pressed together in a firm, unforgiving line. His bangs shifted, exposing his eyes, rimmed with dark circles caused by sleep deprivation and filled with an unmistakable emotion —humiliation.

I stepped forward in an attempt to bridge the gap between us but the guard strong-armed me, briskly reminding me I was not to touch the prisoner. I held my hands up in apology before settling on the nearest bench. Leah gave the guard a hard stare but followed suit. What was that all about? Before I could ask, Charlie sat down across from us, hands and feet in awkward angles to accommodate his wieldy accessories.

We looked at one another in silence until Detective Vargas offered us privacy, noting the guard would be stationed just outside the door, should we need anything. I chuckled to myself as I translated it to "Don't try anything." Ha, as if we'd stage a jail break.

"Charlie…you look…" Once the three of us were alone, I found myself struggling for the right words. How do you tell someone like Charlie that he looked…well, like death?

He sensed my discomfort and elected to complete the thought himself, "Heinous? Barbaric? Like a complete hot mess?" He gave a small, bitter laugh. "Take your pick. I'm fortunate my accommodations lack mirrors."

Leah attempted to lighten the mood. "It seems pretty stingy to me. I'd think my tax dollars would at least warrant a cot, a bedpan, a wash basin and a mirror for primping. You know, the standard jailhouse accoutrement."

Charlie smiled thinly. "They don't want to risk anything that could be broken and used as a weapon on our fellow inmates, or on ourselves."

"Err…yeah, there's that, too," Leah balked as her face flushed. Clearly Charlie wasn't in the mood for witty banter. "So, how are you doing?"

He responded with a long, hooded look. Leah quickly recognized his annoyance and raised her hands in surrender. "Sorry, sorry, just trying to make conversation. Let's not forgot, you summoned us."

He nodded as his gaze traveled to his shackled hands. "The County Attorney is getting ready to formally charge me." He swallowed hard before continuing, "And I need your…help… with some things. Before that happens and before they move me…elsewhere."

"Do you need us to hire a lawyer?" I asked, reaching out but retracting my hand as I remembered the guard's admonishment.

"No, nothing like that. I've got that handled." He smiled wryly, making me wonder who he had retained. Maybe his ex? "Anyway, it seems as though the police and the County Attorney's Office think they've got enough evidence to move forward with first degree murder. They're going for the death penalty." His tone was more glum than distraught, as though telling us Aston Martin had stopped all production for the interminable future.

Leah must have been thinking the same. "Charlie Wilson, they're talking about the death penalty. How can you be so…so lackadaisical?"

Charlie rolled his eyes. "Gee, thanks for that info, Leah. Now that you've cleared things up, I can go back to my cell and watch the cement crack." Leah pursed her lips, not buying his bravado. "Sure, the death penalty or life in prison—either would be dire—if I was guilty."

"The proof they have must be pretty solid if they think they can move forward with formal charges," Leah replied.

"That's true. It's also the reason I asked you both here." He leaned forward, squinting at each of us conspiratorially. "I want you to figure out who killed Parker…and bring him to justice."

* * *

A resounding "no" echoed as we responded in tandem, emphasizing the barrenness of the room. Making casual inquiries was one thing, conducting an actual investigation—on a murder case—was quite another. Had Charlie not received the memo? A conviction would mean his life, one way or the other.

"Charlie, we are not PIs," I gritted out, carefully enunciating each word.

"I don't care," he replied simply.

"We have friends—the Stanton brothers in L.A.—we could hire…professional help from professional investigators who know how to run an investigation. See a theme here, Charlie? And let's not forget the benefits associated with acquiring solid legal counsel." I looked at him squarely. I needed him to listen to me, to hear me.

He shook his head, adamant. "I've thought about it and it's what I want." He must not have liked the look that passed between us, because he tacked on his most sincere "please."

Leah rolled her eyes but nodded. I sighed and did the same. Though we had already done some initial snooping, we were officially graduating to amateur sleuths. Nancy Drew lite, on our best day.

Obviously pleased, Charlie clasped his hands together as a small smile escaped. "Where do we start?"

"Whoa, hold up there, Chuck." Charlie bristled, precisely the reaction Leah had wanted. "We need to set some ground rules if we are going to do this…whatever *this* is."

I agreed. "First, you need to be more forthcoming with the details. A lot more, actually."

"What my friend is saying, Charlie"—Leah gritted out his name—"is that it's time you stop jerkying us around."

"You mean jerking," he replied dryly.

"I mean what I say," she snarked. "I'm the resident word smith, after all."

"What Leah is trying to say is that we need you to be absolutely truthful with us, about everything." I paused to glare at her. She was getting way too much pleasure from torturing Charlie. Even if he deserved it, we were wasting valuable time. Besides, we could prod him with a sharp stick after we got him out of this predicament.

"And we mean everything. If we ask, you answer—truthfully. If you balk, hedge or outright lie, all bets are off. Are we clear?"

Charlie worked his jaw and nodded, before turning to Leah. "To use your analogy, I will refrain from treating you like an old, tough, mangy side of bovine. Just don't blame me if you don't like everything you hear."

"Agreed. We may not like it, but we won't bail on you because of it," Leah replied.

"Ok, then," I clapped, "let's proceed. For starters, do you have any idea what the police have on you? Other than the stuff we already know about, of course."

"Honestly, no, not really," Charlie replied. "It could be anything at this point."

"We understand Natalie was here? What was that all about?" Leah was in reporter mode.

"Not sure, other than to offer her support, I guess," he tapped his chin, "though at one point, she suggested things would be easier if I plead guilty. Of course, she immediately laughed it off, chalking it up as an attempt at humor."

"Wow, that's an unusual way of going about it—kind of insensitive, if you ask me—and frankly, not something I'd expect from her. Did you get the impression she thought you were guilty?"

"She did just lose her boyfriend, you know," his tone was droll, "which might explain her odd behavior. But no, she doesn't think I'm guilty, or at least that's what she indicated, though I'm obviously not a very good judge of people. Present company excluded, of course."

"Any idea who's driving Parker's Audi these days, other than Natalie?" I asked, thinking back to Natalie's mystery ride.

"What? No, no one should be driving Parker's car. There isn't anyone else." He looked perplexed. "Are you sure it was Parker's car and just not one that looked like it? There are other Audi R8s out there."

I shook my head. "Mmm…no, not that many, not in that particular shade of blue, anyway,"

"Sure there is. In fact, Morgan has one, in the same color."

"Morgan, your ex-girlfriend, the lawyer, has an R8?" When he nodded, Leah added, "Ok…but I think I would have noticed a California license plate."

"No, she maintains a dual-residence. Her car is registered in Arizona."

"Ok…is there any reason Natalie and Morgan would be hanging out and Morgan would be acting as Natalie's designated driver?"

Charlie laughed. "Not likely. Morgan doesn't do anything that doesn't benefit Morgan. She wouldn't even offer taxi money to her best friend, much less be expected to be at someone else's beck and call." He shook his head. "Besides, they don't exactly run in the same circles. Morgan thinks Natalie is a dip. No, it must have been another Audi." I disagreed and from the look on Leah's face, she did too—it was too much of a coincidence.

I put the car in park for the time being, electing to move on to another topic. "On the night of the party, why didn't you take your key card when you left the penthouse to take a walk?"

"I don't know. I was distracted and must have misplaced it at some point during the day. It was stupid and so unlike me. I didn't realize it until after the party, but by then I was too tired to mess with it, so I had Stu let me back in." He chuckled softly. "I didn't think it was that big of a deal at the time."

Unfortunately, the police did think it was a big deal and believed Charlie had attempted to establish an alibi by engaging the doorman that night under false pretenses. One thing was for sure, Leah and I would be hard-pressed to prove otherwise without our own evidence. I gritted my teeth. We were so in over our heads.

"What happened to your shoes and tie after the walk?"

Charlie squinted, trying to remember. "My shoes got soaked when I tromped along the lake. Actually, given the amount of alcohol I had that night, I probably spent most of my walk off the pathway. I can't begin to tell you how bad of an idea that turned out to be." Neither of us replied. It had been a bad idea, probably the worst of his life, "When I came back, I went into the parking garage and placed the shoes under the Aston Martin to allow them to dry, along with the socks."

"Using your key code?" Leah prompted.

"Yes, the code is specific to me," he replied. I wondered if the police had checked the activity log for the parking garage and if so, if it meshed with what he was telling us.

Something else occurred to me. "Hang on a second, what about the tie?"

Charlie's expression immediately changed from puzzled to

concerned. "I hadn't realized it was missing. After Stu let me in, I went up and threw everything into the bag for the laundry service to pick up the following morning."

Stu hadn't been sure about the tie, either and yet Natalie had found one near the lake. Had it been Parker's? Or Charlie's? There was no sense pursuing the issue at this point—Charlie would likely never remember anyway, given the amount of alcohol he'd had—we'd need to rely on the security videos to fill in the blanks.

Thinking of the videos reminded me of something else. "You mentioned the penthouse cameras to Leah. Does Arch know about them?"

Charlie smiled thinly. "He knows about the cameras I want him to know about."

"Such as…" Leah was getting impatient with the brevity of his responses. I couldn't say I blamed her, time was of the essence.

"The cameras placed throughout the main portion of the building, including the entrance and parking garage."

"Not the cameras inside the penthouse?"

"Of course not," Charlie snarked, "that would defeat the purpose."

"Careful, Charlie Brown…" Leah snapped. "We didn't come here for your attitude." Charlie glared at her and opened his mouth to retort.

"Play nice, kids," I interjected. "What about audio?"

Charlie shook his head. "Currently, the penthouse's cameras are the only ones set up to capture sound."

"Can we get access to that feed? Stu was able to supply us with everything but—" I snapped my mouth shut, hoping I hadn't gotten the doorman into trouble.

Charlie waved his hand, apparently not concerned by my comment. "Certainly, I'll give you the name and number of my security expert. He's more of a computer and audio visual geek, but he's a genius with pretty much anything tech-related." As Leah jotted the information down, he added, "You didn't happen to check on the penthouse while you were there talking to Stu, did you? Not that I have any plants or pets, but I'm hoping the cops didn't make a total mess."

I gave Leah an uh-oh glance, which Charlie caught. There was no good time to tell him about the suspected penthouse squatter. He worked his jaw as we told him about Arch and the inhabited guest room.

"You want us to boot him?" Leah asked when we finished, sounding a tad too hopeful.

"No," Charlie replied slowly, thinking as he spoke, "this could actually work out to our advantage. It will allow us…you…to keep an eye on him, meaning you should contact my security guy sooner rather than later."

"Speaking of that, he's not going to give up the goods based on our say so." Leah had a good point.

"No, you'll have to give him the secret handshake, followed by a blood oath." Charlie chuckled at our horrified expressions. "Just give him your nickname, AJ," he winked at me, "that's the password."

I was too startled to respond before the guard entered, informing us the visit was over. As we parted ways, I turned and looked back at Charlie shuffling in the opposite direction under heavy-handed guidance.

"Charlie!" I shouted, causing the guard's perma-frown to deepen. "What is Natalie to you?"

Charlie glanced over his shoulder in surprise as his handler continued to propel him forward. "What?" he managed to sputter. "Natalie? Nothing—a friend, if that."

They disappeared through the double doors. If Charlie had

been prepared to elaborate, he'd lost his chance. I wondered if he had been relieved.

As we collected Nicoh from the desk sergeant, I realized Detective Vargas had not returned to escort us out. Given Leah's sour expression, she noticed as well. I started to comment, when I observed the sergeant was in an equally bitter mood.

"What's the matter?"

He thrust Nicoh's lead at me. "What's the matter? I left my sandwich on the desk to take a call. My back was turned…oh, I don't know…three seconds? I finished the call, went to eat my sandwich and…it…was…gone." It was all I could do not to giggle.

Leah opted to bat her baby blues. "Any chance the wind blew it away?"

I bit my tongue and shot her a pithy look before turning to the sergeant. "I'm so, so sorry. I usually chalk it up to hazard duty. Please let me buy you another lunch. We could run down to Mill Street and grab you another sandwich, or up to Oregano's on University?"

The sergeant shook his head and waved a hand, though I could tell he was still miffed. "I truly appreciate the offer, Miss. Honestly, I'm not mad your dog ate my lunch. It's that he inhaled it so fast, he didn't even bother to enjoy it." He wiggled a finger at Nicoh, whose tongue dangled happily as he scouted for dessert.

"Welcome to my world, Sergeant."

CHAPTER THIRTEEN

Running interference for Charlie was proving to be a lot more time-consuming than either Leah or I had imagined, we mused as we checked our missed messages.

One text in particular caught my eye: *YOU MIGHT BE ABLE TO SAVE YOUR FRIEND, ARIANNA, BUT WILL YOU BE ABLE TO SAVE YOURSELF?* Well…crap. Apparently this person wasn't a member of the Arianna Jackson fan club after all. I handed my cell to Leah after she tucked Nicoh into the back seat.

After reading it, her mouth formed a thin line. "Call Ramirez —now."

She drove as I dialed, putting my cell on speakerphone. He picked up on the first ring and after a few niceties, I filled him in on my latest mystery text.

"Darn it, AJ," he growled, once I had finished.

"Tell me about it. Was your contact able to come up with anything?"

"Not yet, other than our caller is into using throwaway phones."

"So what's AJ supposed to do in the meantime—wait until this guy escalates to anthrax-laced greeting cards?"

I patted my friend's knee. "I doubt anything like that is going to happen."

Ramirez's response surprised me, "Leah's right to be concerned. You're going to need to be more careful, watch your surroundings and if anything seems out of place—no matter how insignificant—call me." Though I couldn't see his face, his tone indicated he wasn't about to take "no" for an answer. "And, at least for a while, I'd like the two…three…of you to stick together, if at all possible. The more eyes we have on deck, the better."

"I have no idea what that means." Leah snorted. "So that's it, then? Just stick to AJ like glue, grow eyes in the back of our heads, attach a beacon to Nicoh and wait until this jerk rears his crazy head? For how long are we supposed to do this, anyway? Until we become crotchety old maids bickering about our bad 80s hair days?"

"Considering you're already pretty crabby, I guess all you'll need to contend with is your questionable hair choices over the years." I snickered under my breath as Ramirez teased my friend.

"Hey, wait just a minute—if you weren't a cop…"

"A homicide detective," I added helpfully.

"Whatever. I just wish there was something more proactive we could do," she conceded, but not before sticking her tongue out at me. "Since we've already got your ear, Detective Ramirez, we'd like to pick your brain about Charlie's case."

"I thought I asked you to stay out of it," his tone was no longer jovial. "Besides, why not hit up your TPD source, unless he's already shut you down, too?"

She made a face at the phone. "A girl's gotta keep her bases covered, no sense spreading myself too thin. Even a detective should understand that. Oh well, I just thought your poker buddy was keeping you in the loop. Guess I was wrong about that."

At Ramirez's grumbled response—I won't repeat it verbatim, other than to say it involved tossing a particular region of her anatomy into the brig—I quickly intercepted by highlighting our findings. I hoped sharing the information we'd discovered first might open the exchange of information. After a brief outline of our conversations with Stuart, Arch and Charlie, my gamble worked.

Ramirez was quiet for a moment before responding, "The Tempe boys have copies of the camera feed, though given the range of dates they're reviewing, I'm not sure how far they've gotten." His tone indicated he wasn't about to share what had been found to date, but I got the distinct impression from what he hadn't said TPD had found something. I hoped it wasn't more bad news for Charlie. Before I had the opportunity to comment, Ramirez abruptly ended the conversation, citing an urgent matter needing his attention.

"That was evasive," Leah commented as we stared at my cell phone. "Makes me glad we kept a few juicy details to ourselves."

"You don't suppose Vargas would be any more forthcoming, do you?"

"Heck no, I've already run that tab higher than even I'm comfortable doing. Pretty soon, he's going to want to cash in on some of that good will."

"So, you don't like him?" I was curious.

"It's not that I don't like Vargas…Jere…I just don't care for his baggage."

"Err, come again?"

"His ex. Baggage. Call her Samsonite, as in she doesn't fit well in the overhead bins."

"Ah," I nodded in understanding, though it wasn't like my friend to throw in the towel so easily. Girl typically liked the challenge, so it had to be something else. "He's still hung up on her?" I ventured a guess.

"No, it's that I *know* her."

"She's still around?"

She laughed harshly. "You could say that. She was one of my former editors at the paper and the primary reason I left. A jealous, vindictive boss tends to evaporate the creative juices." At my surprised look, she waved a hand. "Heck, I was ready for a change anyway."

I was floored. I thought she'd left the paper, given up her condo and moved in with me because she needed a fresh start after being kidnapped and nearly murdered by Winslow Clark. I'd had no idea one of her bosses had also been making her work life hell, simply because she could.

No, I couldn't imagine Leah losing the choice assignments she had worked so hard for or being forced to work in vile or unsafe locations. It was likely more than she could bear. And after she'd given up so much: security, control, piece of mind.

"Oh Leah, I'm so sorry. I didn't know."

She waved a hand at me. "You already had a lot of your own stuff to deal with—the death of your parents and your sister—you didn't need to deal with my crap, too. Besides, leaving that mess behind turned out to be the best and most profitable decision I ever made. Anyway, now you know why Detective Jere Vargas and I can never be more than friends. And a source of information, of course." She smiled and patted my leg. "Why don't we find out what those cameras captured? I'll bet watching the videos TPD has will even up that information playing field."

"And the videos *inside* the penthouse will put us a step ahead." We both giggled conspiratorially.

Darn, I knew we were best friends for a reason.

* * *

Tony Barbados, a.k.a. Tony B.—Charlie's security expert/audio video/computer geek extraordinaire—picked up on the first ring sounding harried and if I wasn't mistaken, more than a little paranoid. Fortunately, after explaining my reason for calling and giving him the secret handshake—my nickname, Ajax—Tony B. chilled as much as I imagined a guy on a Red Bull-fortified diet could muster. His voice fluctuated as he energetically explained how to go about accessing the video feed via my laptop. After a few dozen strokes, I was in. I thanked Tony B. repeatedly for his assistance, but he made noises into the phone that indicated he was more interested into getting back to whatever geeky evil genius types did.

After hanging up, I filled Leah in and suggested we make an afternoon out of watching the videos. This meant procuring the appropriate snacks. While Leah made popcorn—on the stove, of course—I started putting together a snack tray when the doorbell rang.

Upon peering through the keyhole, I was surprised to find Randy Newman—not *that* Randy Newman—my neighbor from around the corner looking back. Thanks to Nicoh's happy dance on my foot, I knew Randy had his Keeshond, Pandora, in tow and after a few howls and small yips were exchanged through the door, the two were united.

Though he'd originally retired at the ripe old age of thirty-eight, Randy had recently returned to the world of corporate law in a position that required moderate travel. We'd become acquainted while out walking our dogs in the neighborhood, as well as on the occasions when Pandora had escaped and made her way into my yard. As a result, we had become friendly to the point he felt comfortable leaving her in my care when his job took him out of town. I suspected it was the reason for his current visit.

Randy blushed as we joined Leah in the kitchen. I'd always believed that—much like Abe Stanton—he had a bit of a crush on her and had told her as much, though she vehemently denied it. Randy was definitely a nice, well-mannered guy and decent looking to boot, with sandy hair, deep tan and athletic build honed from years of tennis. Unfortunately, the only thing Randy loved more than his work was talking about it.

Needless to say, it was one of Leah's dating non-negotiables. I could hardly say I blamed her, though I did feel sorry for Randy. He had it bad for Leah and though he was normally a pretty talkative guy, became a rambling fool around our little spiky-haired pixie. And, after a few embarrassing episodes, he started clamping up whenever she was in the vicinity. Today, he was content with leaning against the counter, watching her make popcorn.

"So, are you heading out of town again, Randy?"

"Oh, yeah…sorry," he momentarily peeled his eyes from Leah's activity, exciting as it was, "it's kind of short notice, but one of my clients in Dallas needs some hand-holding."

"Say no more, I'd be happy to watch Pandora. Wouldn't we, Nicoh?" The two canines were doing their customary sniff-and-wag bit, oblivious to the humans in the room. I opened the sliding doors that lead to the backyard patio, "Out of the kitchen, you two. You can do…that…outside." They ran out in tandem, barking and nipping at each other's tails.

Randy left for the airport with a promise to call with his return plans, leaving Leah and I to finish our snack preparations. Once completed, we enthusiastically made our way to the living room to convene the video watching portion of our investigation. As it turned out, the security footage of Charlie's building was B-O-R-I-N-G. People came. People went. People did what people do. For hours, nothing out of the ordinary occurred or was even remotely interesting.

I realized I'd lost Leah when a small snore came from the section of the cushions where she'd burrowed, one hand still draped in the popcorn bowl. As I got up to move it, I almost missed a segment of video that showed Natalie entering the building. I noted the time on the feed—it was during the period I'd been in the penthouse setting up for the White Party. I watched as she exited, less than five minutes later.

I opened my laptop and logged into the penthouse's video links as Tony B. had directed. Several keystrokes later, I was looking at the entryway to Charlie's penthouse, a few minutes prior to the time indicated on the feed from the building. For a moment I felt kind of voyeuristic, but quickly pushed the squishy thought aside as Charlie appeared, moving quickly through the entryway and onto the elevator—likely on his way to the meeting he still wouldn't discuss. I had forgotten there was sound on this video and adjusted it a couple of levels above Leah's snores.

Less than fifteen minutes passed before Arch came into view and sat at his desk—whether he realized Charlie had left, I wasn't sure—and shortly after that, Natalie stepped off the elevator. I checked the timestamp on the video from the building's entrance —a little more than a minute has passed—the time it took to ride the elevator to the penthouse.

Natalie appraised Arch for a moment, her face devoid of its usual perkiness, and her pouty lips in a grim line. "Do you have what I came for, or what?" she snapped.

"I do…" Arch replied slowly, twirling his fingers in a circular pattern over the steel surface, his own expression smug. *What the heck?* I thought.

"I don't have all day." Natalie thrust out her hand expectantly.

"Before I hand this over, I want some assurances." He smiled coyly.

"Listen, you little freak," she gritted out, her features turning dark—hardly recognizable from the pretty, polite girl I knew. Her finger prodded his chest. "We had a deal, buddy. So either you give me what I came for—"

"Or what, Natalie?" Arch remained surprisingly calm, more amused than angered as he enunciated her name in an effort to taunt her.

"Or I let Charlie know what you've been up to." Her smile transformed into a sneer—neither had been attractive on her.

Arch shifted slightly, but smirked as they glared at one another. After a long moment, he slid something across the desk, which she easily palmed and placed into her monstrosity of a handbag. She spun on her heel and without looking back, called to him as she entered the elevator, "I was never here."

Arch replied, his voice sharp, "Just remember, we had a deal. I want no part of the rest of it."

Natalie turned, carefully inching cat-eye sunglasses up her nose, her eyes piercing his. As the elevator doors slid shut, her voice was barely a whisper, but the meaning was clear, "Oh, I remember, Archy Boy. I remember…everything."

CHAPTER FOURTEEN

I quickly rewound the tape and tried several dozen times to zoom in on whatever it was Arch had given her, but it was masked by their hands as it passed between them. It was so frustrating. I put a few choice expletives out into the universe loudly enough to wake Leah, who ended up knocking over the popcorn bowl I had removed from her slumbering clutches.

"Crap." She squinted, frowning as she tried to focus. "Did you drink all the margaritas, or what?"

I laughed so hard I snorted. "Wrong dream, Sunshine. No margaritas here."

Leah grumbled, throwing pillows, stray popcorn kernels, a few gummy bears and at least one Sour Patch Kid as she attempted to reposition herself on the couch.

After I managed to contain myself, I added, "Sorry, I interrupted your nap, but now that you're awake, I found something interesting on the video the morning before the party. Here, maybe I should just show you." I adjusted the videos to the same timestamp and once Leah gave me a nod, started them both.

The audio boomed, causing us to cover our ears in surprise.

"Why in the heck is that so darn loud?" Leah cried as I scrambled to adjust the audio.

"Because I was trying to hear over your snoring," I replied dryly.

"I do not snore. I have sinus issues." She sniffed indignantly while waving at me in a *let's get on with it* manner.

After a successful second attempt, we watched the scene between Natalie and Arch. When the elevator doors closed on Natalie's death glare, Leah stopped the recording. "And we thought Parker was the ruthless one. Any idea what that was?" she asked, pointing to the item that passed between them.

I shook my head. "Not a clue. I even tried to zoom in but it was too small and conveniently concealed."

"Are we sure that Arch doesn't know about that camera?"

"Charlie says no, but at this point I don't think we can afford to discount the possibility."

"How the heck do they even know each other? Like *that*, I mean."

"I have no idea, but whatever is going on certainly doesn't give you a warm fuzzy."

"Totally agree with you, but we're going to have to scrounge up more than that"—she gestured toward the screen—"to prove something mischievous is afoot."

"Let's hope we can find something of value on the remainder these videos, provided you can manage to stay awake." A piece of candy bounced off my head. "Just say 'no' to gummy bear abuse, Leah."

We returned our attention to the video, where nothing of interest occurred until after I'd finished my setup duties and left the penthouse. A short while later, Charlie's Aston Martin entered the parking garage and maneuvered into his space. Upon exiting the car, Charlie looked up at the camera and immediately pulled his cell phone from his pocket. After a brief call, all the parking garage feeds simultaneously went blank. I glanced at Leah—at least Charlie had been truthful about one thing—he'd definitely disabled the cameras.

Minutes later, he was visible on the penthouse feed as he exited the elevator, a healthy frown emerging as he saw Arch at his post.

"I've temporarily disabled the cameras in the parking garage as Senator Conrad requested, so he and his entourage may come and go unnoticed."

"Ok," Arch replied slowly, "doesn't that mean dismantling the security on your vehicles and the other resident's vehicles, too?"

"Yes," Charlie snapped, "there's nothing I can do about that. It had to be done, and now it is. That's all you need to know. Got it?" It wasn't a question. "Of course, if something happens to Conrad's car while it's in the structure, it's on him."

"Oh, I would think the senator has people to take care of stuff like that, don't you?" Arch replied in an attempt to be helpful. Of course, it had the opposite effect, as Charlie whirled on him.

Arch quickly nodded. "Of course he does. Then…why…why did he request to have the security cameras turned off?"

Both Leah and I blanched as Charlie's expression turned from irritated to irate. "Arch, I get the impression you are purposely trying to test my patience today. Bad idea." Arch backed up, just a little, though I doubted Charlie registered the movement, given the blackness of his mood. "The senator will be bringing some special…guests to the party. Guests that will be arriving with his entourage, but aren't to be seen accompanying him, if you get my meaning?" He spun on his heal and marched toward the kitchen.

I looked at Leah, even if Arch hadn't gotten it, we certainly had. If the rumors about former Senator Davis Conrad were true, they would be special *female* guests, other than his wife. It wasn't until we watched him watching Charlie's departure we realized Arch wasn't the stooge everyone thought him to be.

As he stared after his boss, a tiny smile escaped.

* * *

Considering Arch had just gotten his job back, you would have thought he'd avoid aggravating Charlie. Yet here he was, clearly putting his foot into it, and enjoying it. Charlie was wrong—Arch wasn't a nitwit. He was a manipulator. He'd played on Charlie's impatient, arrogant nature to get a rise out of him and possibly, some valuable information. The question was why? And for what purpose? While Arch had done a decent job of playing Charlie, he wasn't a murderer, much less the facilitator of one. Something told me whatever he was up to, it wasn't good.

The last scene had given us something to gnaw on, but it wasn't enough. We continued to watch as Arch went back to his duties, which consisted of organizing his sparsely-covered desk in an attempt to appear as though he was performing meaningful work. Amusing, but boring.

Not having to deal with the parking garage videos was certainly a plus, but even screening the others at a faster speed was time-consuming. At times, it was humorous—especially watching ourselves arrive for the party all decked out in white, tugging here and there, while bickering back and forth in double time. Once the guests finally started arriving for the White Party, however, we returned the playback to its normal speed, paying especially close attention to Natalie's arrival.

We couldn't read lips, though it appeared she had transformed back to her girl-next-door persona, making polite small talk with Stu while she waited for Parker. When he arrived several minutes later, Parker ignored the doorman while giving Natalie's ensemble a disapproving perusal. Natalie, however, seemed oblivious to his gaze—or had grown used to it—as she giggled and threaded her arm through his. Parker impatiently ushered her onto the elevator, which made me wonder if she was an exceptional actress, or genuinely happy to be in his company. My gut told me one thing while my gag reflux was threatening another.

Watching the rest of the party play out—including Charlie's snub of Parker—was surreal and frankly, a bit bizarre, especially when seeing your own reaction. You never look quite the way you imagined, do you?

I was also struck by the realization these were likely the last moments of Parker's life. It no longer mattered he'd spent it as an egotistical, self-serving jerk. It had been his life to live, good or bad. And yet, on this night, someone decided the ending of his story for him. In a few short hours, Parker would be dead. That alone was the most surreal, and sobering fact.

Charlie's ex, Morgan, entered the party next, looking every ounce as gorgeous as I remembered but…

"Leah, she never entered the building though the main entrance—she never passed Stuart!"

"What? I missed it." We reversed the playback and sure enough—prior to the point we had witnessed Morgan emerge from the elevator—she hadn't entered the building through the main entrance. She had come in another way.

"She's one of Senator Conrad's special guests," I whispered.

"No!" Leah pointed excitedly. "She *is* the senator's special guest." Moments after Morgan had passed through the entryway alone, the elevators reopened and the man himself stepped out… also very alone.

"Whoa, do you think Charlie knew…that his ex and the senator…and that was the reason he was so short with Arch?"

"I don't know, but I don't think it matters." I tapped my chin thoughtfully, "What matters is that *she* knew."

"Err, I don't follow," Leah crinkled her nose at me, "of course Morgan would know…"

"No, Leah, she knew the security cameras would be disabled

in the parking garage."

We continued watching in silence as the party droned on and people drank, cavorted and did what people generally do when they've imbibed too much. But other than some sidebar silliness that occurred when people thought no one was watching, nothing more of interest happened.

From our perspective, Morgan and the senator had limited to no interaction. When she eventually left the party, however, her escort left shortly after. As expected, neither made an exit through the front of the building. Instead, the elevator had taken each of them to the parking structure, where they were able to steal away unnoticed.

Leah and I had left the party by that time, along with several other guests. I strained to find a glimpse of Charlie among the partygoers, but wherever he was, the cameras were out of reach. My attention was drawn to Parker and Natalie leaving the party, then exiting the building minutes later. As they slipped into the night, I again reflected on the moment being the last record of his life.

It was a shame Charlie had dismantled the security cameras in the parking garage, a fact the police were likely having a field day with. And knowing Charlie as I did, he'd probably failed to mention the former senator's request, making their case stronger and his situation worse. Even if he had, I doubted Senator Conrad would have corroborated the claim. Charlie had gotten himself into a real pickle this time.

The party continued to wind down as guests left and Charlie finally came into view. I quickly realized he had been in the atrium, one of the few areas—along with the bedrooms and bathrooms—devoid of cameras. As he walked the last of the guests to the elevator and wished them good night, he seemed genuinely pleased as a small smile formed. It didn't quite reach his eyes, indicating his mind was elsewhere.

The smile evaporated as Arch appeared and while still facing the elevators, Charlie spoke to his assistant in a hushed, raspy voice, "Would you mind telling the staff they can go for now?"

"Are you sure? "Arch stammered, clearly taken aback by his boss' directive. "There's a lot of clean up to be done."

Charlie waved off his concern, his back still to his assistant. "It's fine. It all can be done…later. Can you coordinate that?" he asked quietly, while Arch nodded. As though sensing the affirmation, he added, "Thank you. After that, you should go ahead and take off, too. Get some rest. You'll be back soon enough."

Arch started to say something but must have thought better of it, silently returning to the kitchen to confer with the staff. When Charlie turned around, an undecipherable expression spanned his face, as he trudged toward master bedroom,

Arch and the others were gone by the time he emerged. His jacket was off and his tie loose as he looked around solemnly, reaching into the pocket of his slacks. Frowning, he reached into the other pocket, then muttered in frustration as he flipped off the remaining lights and entered the elevator. He reappeared on the building video as he stopped to talk with Stu before leaving through the front entrance.

He returned, over an hour later. As he and Stu had both indicated, he was neither wearing nor carrying his shoes. Also missing was the tie. And though he appeared even more tired than before, he looked just like the Charlie we'd seen leaving the building. There was no evidence—physical or otherwise—he'd been in a struggle, much less murdered his best friend.

We watched until he entered the penthouse and headed toward his bedroom before fast-forwarding to the point when Arch arrived to begin his workday a few short hours later, followed by the party cleanup crew.

At 9 a.m., Charlie emerged from his room with a laundry bag in hand just as an elderly man, dressed neatly in a short sleeve shirt and chinos exited the elevator. Few words were exchanged before the man left, laundry bag in hand. Arch was overseeing the cleanup crew in another part of the penthouse, which explained why he'd missed the transaction that morning.

After another hour of yawning and capturing nothing of value, we took a break to document a few of the questions we had accumulated to this point.

Question #1—What had Arch handed to Natalie? It was obvious Charlie had been missing his key card—was that it? If so, why had she taken it?

Question #2—What was going on between Arch and Natalie? How did they know one another (other than through Charlie)?

Question #3—Did they know who killed Parker? Or have any knowledge that might help Charlie?

Question #4—Morgan and the former senator had known the parking garage cameras would be disabled that evening. Had they shared that information with anyone?

Question #5—How did Parker end up in the parking garage? Natalie had taken a cab—leaving Parker to walk to his own car. Had he ever made it that far? What happened to him between the time Natalie left him and the time he was killed? Was he lured somehow? Had he already planned to meet someone?

Question #6—Why hadn't Natalie mentioned seeing his car when she went back to get hers?

Question #7—Could one person feasibly incapacitate, kill and dump someone Parker's size?

As expected, we had more questions than answers and of the people that could provide them, we weren't convinced they would. One thing was for sure, we weren't prepared to deal with Natalie. Not yet, anyway. She had been fairly unpredictable during our previous discussions and after what we'd seen of her in the video footage, maybe even a bit devious. No, before we dealt with her again, we'd need more ammunition. The same was true of Arch. As for Senator Conrad, good luck cracking that nut. We'd likely end up spending valuable time and yielding minimal results. Plus, we'd have to explain our knowledge of the dismantled camera, which would divulge information only Charlie should have known. That left Morgan, Charlie's ex and the former senator's mystery guest.

Unfortunately, tracking Morgan Thompson down turned out to be more difficult than we had anticipated. Upon calling the law firm in San Francisco where she served as a partner, we were promptly informed Morgan had recently taken a leave of absence to attend to a family matter and had not left a private number where she could be reached.

Leah managed to work her magic and after a few phone calls and a whole lot of grousing, was able to obtain what we believed to be Morgan's personal cell phone number. Of course, now that we had it, we couldn't exactly call her and ask her outright if she was Senator Davis Conrad's mistress. We needed information, not to confirm some seedy gossip, and decided the best way to go about it was on the pretense of locating character references to aid in Charlie's defense.

I was elected to make the call after losing the gummy bear toss—neither of us had any coins—and was surprised when Morgan picked up after two short rings, sounding breathless. Thinking I had gotten the wrong number or that Morgan had some interesting side business going, I considered hanging up when she quickly apologized, explaining she had a habit of answering phone calls during her daily run. I, too, apologized for my interruption and quickly detailed my reason for touching base with a few of Charlie's friends.

Morgan laughed harshly, clearly amused. "Charlie doesn't have *friends*, darling. He has acquisitions." She paused a moment before adding, "He's just lucky we live in the desert, otherwise he'd be hard-pressed to keep himself warm at night." I wasn't surprised by what she said, it was how she said it that spoke volumes, in the Encyclopedia Britannia kind of way. That and something else piqued my attention.

"So, you're living here now?"

She chuckled, her tone much lighter. "It's just an expression, darling. When you are born and raised in Phoenix, the Valley of the Sun is always part of you, no matter where your physical home resides." I quirked an eyebrow at Leah, currently biting her lip as she was forced to sit back and listen via speakerphone. "Besides, my parents still live here."

It was news to us. Neither of us had realized Morgan was from Arizona, much less from right in our own backyard. It was surprising that Charlie had never mentioned it. It was definitely worth looking into.

As Leah furiously jotted in her trusty notebook, Morgan and I made small talk about Charlie's party—carefully avoiding the topic of her escort for the evening—as well as Parker's death and the ongoing investigation. She didn't believe Charlie killed Parker, or had any involvement. When I asked if she could drum up any other likable candidates or possible motives, her mood darkened.

"Arianna, Charlie and Parker...are not good people. Charlie could have been killed, just as easily as Parker and no one would have cared, much less cried. Tears spill *because* of those two, not *for* them. As for motives, it would be easier to identify what wouldn't have been a motive. It's a short list." She sighed heavily before hanging up, leaving me to wonder if this was the tale of a scorned and bitter ex-girlfriend, or the reality of someone who'd experienced Charlie and Parker's world first hand.

Either way, it was clear that while Morgan believed Charlie was not responsible for killing Parker, in the end she felt they were both getting exactly what they deserved.

CHAPTER FIFTEEN

I'll admit, we didn't have much of a game plan after talking to Morgan, so I shouldn't have been surprised Leah's expression was one of horror when I placed a spontaneous call to Natalie the following afternoon. Something about my chat with Morgan had inspired me and sometimes, you've gotta trust your gut. I only hoped my instincts hadn't gotten confused by the overabundance of Sour Patch Kids currently rumbling around in my tummy.

"You just invited…Natalie…over…for drinks," Leah commented slowly, after I'd hung up. "Natalie."

I shrugged. "I guess we'd better move the potted plants."

Natalie promptly arrived an hour later. Seeing her fresh face and perky smile, it was hard to rationalize her snarling exchange with Arch as she hugged us and presented us with Costco-sized bottles of tequila and margarita mixer and enough limes to make me think she must have foraged someone's backyard tree. The girl came armed and ready.

Natalie moaned as she tested Leah's cilantro lime jalapeño hummus on a baby carrot and tried bribing her for the recipe as I fed Nicoh and Pandora and got them situated for the evening.

Though the two knew the routine, I had to scold their repeated attempts to inch closer to the activity in the living room.

Natalie giggled as she watched me giving Nicoh the stink-eye, "I've wanted to get together like this for so long."

"Get together, with us?" Leah asked curiously.

"Well, sure. We did all go to high school together and have mutual friends. We should have done this ages ago," she replied. We nodded and munched in silence, both of us contemplating the best way of approaching our questions now that we'd lured our guest here. We need not have worried, Natalie initiated the conversation for us.

"It's something about Charlie, huh?" I started to wonder if the girl was psychic as she casually settled into an overstuffed arm chair. "All that evidence. I hear the County Attorney is actually getting ready to formally charge him with murder one. It's all pretty crazy, if you ask me." I wondered where she was getting her inside information.

Apparently, Leah was thinking the same thing, "Huh, that's interesting. What have you heard?"

Natalie leaned forward, her eyes bright as she shared her scoop. "A friend of mine at the County Attorney's Office said they have evidence placing Charlie in the garage at the time Parker was impaled with Big Bess." I winced at her callous choice of phrasing. "Plus, Charlie's admitted to disabling the security cameras in the garage prior to the party. He made up some excuse about doing work on the Eldorado he didn't want recorded, then the car turns out to be the murder weapon. Kind of sloppy, if you ask me."

Leah and I nodded, even though we knew the real reason Charlie had dismantled those cameras, but until we could confirm who was to be trusted, we weren't sharing.

"Anyway, he claims he forgot to turn them back on, meaning

they were off during the party and therefore, during the time Parker conveniently wandered into the parking garage to meet his demise. I mean, who writes this stuff?

"Another thing—no one else had access to Big Bess. It's not like someone would take the time to hotwire an old car like that just so they could murder someone with it. Which didn't happen, by the way." Upon seeing our raised brows, Natalie elaborated, "My friend said the techs tested for that. The car was started with a key, which only one person had access to." She formed a "C" with her thumb and forefinger.

"Err, that all seems pretty circumstantial…" Leah started to comment but Natalie held up a finger.

"Oh, there's more, girlfriend. The shoe and tie I found at the lake were Charlie's…not Parker's, as I had originally thought, though they did dredge his up later. Yuck, I'd bet no amount of OxiClean would get those stains out." She appeared amused by her own rather insensitive joke, making me wonder if she'd changed her mind about Charlie's innocence. The way this conversation was going, it certainly seemed to be the case.

"What about Charlie's claim he placed them in the garage after his walk by the lake?" I asked, assuming her source had already shared whatever specifics the police had gathered.

"Oh, he was there all right, but it wasn't to deposit his shoes. A witness puts Charlie at the entrance of the parking garage during the time they've established Parker was murdered. She said he was cursing at the security panel."

"I thought Charlie turned the security cameras off in the parking garage?"

"The cameras yes, but not the entry keypad. You still had to have a code to get into the garage. Charlie was probably too drunk to remember his, or kept fat-fingering it, because it was the theatrics of his outburst that made him stand out to the woman," Natalie added.

"She's a resident in his building?" Leah asked hopefully.

"I'm not sure about that. All I know is she was out walking her dog."

"Walking her dog at that hour? Interesting," I commented with a sarcastic undertone that only Leah caught.

She rolled her eyes before turning to Natalie. "The friend at the County Attorney's Office you mentioned—the one who gave you the inside track on the investigation—it isn't Sherman, is it? Because some of the details—"

"Oh yes, you know him too?" Natalie seemed pleased by their shared acquaintance.

"Yes, Sherman's been quite helpful in the past, definitely a source you want to have in your bag of tricks," Leah tilted her head slightly as she replied, as though something had aroused her curiosity.

"You got that right," Natalie replied, eager to continue. "He also told me the security log corroborates the witness' account. Apparently, each person has their own unique key code and Charlie's was used at the time the witness puts him at the parking garage's entrance."

"Which puts him in the vicinity of the garage during the time they think Parker was killed," Leah groaned.

"Maybe Charlie gave the key code to someone else?" I thought of the arrangements he had made with Senator Conrad.

"Except he didn't," Natalie replied earnestly, "or at least he said he didn't. Besides, it hadn't been used since he disabled the cameras." My heart sank—Charlie had probably given the senator and his entourage other key codes to use that evening.

Natalie prattled on, "The video of his reentry into the building also fits within their timeframe of the crime. Meaning between the time he returned to the building without his tie and shoes and the witness placed him at the parking garage, Charlie had plenty of leeway to kill Parker in the garage, dump his body and the evidence in the lake." When finished, she opened her hands in apology but her vibe indicated otherwise.

"Hold up a minute, Natalie. Let's assume Charlie had the means and opportunity—what's his motive? We are talking about premeditation after all, which assumes Charlie had planned to kill Parker. Over what—a few lousy deals? Charlie would have been mad—yes. Inconvenienced—yes. But, murderous?" Natalie's expression told me she wasn't buying what I was selling, but honestly, I didn't care. It wasn't Natalie I needed to convince. "I don't know much about law, but I thought, at a minimum, it took means, motive and opportunity to prove someone guilty of first degree murder. In my book, this case isn't quite as open and shut as the County Attorney thinks. Or I don't know Charlie."

Leah nodded. "I agree with AJ. Their rationale just doesn't hold water and without motive, you've got a lopsided wagon."

Natalie stiffened, obviously feeling challenged, though it hadn't been our intention. We were just having a friendly get-together, right?

"I can't answer that. No one but Charlie can. Maybe the business stuff was bigger than we thought? Maybe there were… other…more far-reaching implications?" I shrugged at Leah. We had no idea where Natalie was going with that thought.

Sensing she'd lost us, Natalie waved a white paper towel. "Hey guys, enough of this heavy stuff, who's up for some tasty snacks?" After Leah and I quickly thrust our hands up in the air, a giggle broke through and Natalie relaxed, obviously pleased about the change in topic.

For the next several hours, we ate, gossiped and giggled. During a more raucous bout of laughter, Nicoh and Pandora used the distraction to slink in and nab stray crumbs, but their less than stealthy attempts made the outbursts even more boisterous. Leah took the opportunity to announce it was time to claim our *Real Housewives of Phoenix* taglines, starting us off with hers.

"People say I dig up dirt, but it just tells me they've got something to hide." She finished it off by pimping her best pucker face.

Though Natalie and I could barely contain ourselves, I managed to chime in, "Think of me as a modern day da Vinci—the lens is my canvas and with it, I create masterpieces." I got up and did a little jig, a cross between the Cabbage Patch and Churnin' Butter, putting the other two into further hysterics.

It was Natalie's turn. "People say I'm as sweet as apple pie, but honey don't you dare compare me to baked goods."

We continued to snort and squeal with girlish laughter until Nicoh howled at the top of his lungs, his way of imploring us to stop. Pandora wasn't sure what to make of the situation and took cover under a nearby coffee table. After we'd suitably calmed ourselves, I was able to coax her out and placed her gently on my lap while Nicoh looked on with concern and perhaps a bit of jealously. He'd never been much of a lap top. At ninety-eight pounds, go figure.

Natalie yawned, and after looking at her watch, announced she needed to get a move on. It was a school night for all of us. We offered to call her a cab but she waved us off, noting a girlfriend had dropped her off and was ready to pick her up at a moment's notice. She quickly hugged us, scratched both pups and was down the drive before we had the opportunity to walk her out.

Leah started to say something but I grabbed her arm, pulled her through the door and down the steps, carefully tucking in behind a hedge of bougainvilleas that lined the pathway. Prickly little suckers. A car door opened and we could hear Natalie's tinkling laugh. We peered around the shrub in time to see a familiar blue Audi slip into the night. Its license plate read 4JUSTIS. Charlie had been right—it wasn't Parker's car—though it could very well have belonged to a particular female attorney.

"That alone may have been an interesting culmination to the

evening's events," Leah thumbed in the direction of the Audi, "but Natalie's friend, Sherman, in the County Attorney's Office? Is *Lisa* Sherman…and I'm pretty sure she's still a girl."

CHAPTER SIXTEEN

Why had Natalie been so forthcoming, only to lie about the source of her information? And, if she lied about that, what else had she lied about? After another fitful night, I padded down the hall in my Powerpuff Girl slippers, grumpily noting the superhero powers hadn't started kicking in yet. I was barely recharged and ready to tackle those questions, not to mention the dozens of others Leah and I had somehow managed to accumulate.

I hoped Leah had a more restful night. Even Nicoh and Pandora had seemed content, gently snoozing side by side on his king-sized pet bed until they escaped to the outdoors during the early morning hours. I looked out the window and found them sunning themselves by the pool, belly-sides up. Quite a pair, those two. It would be hard to separate them when Randy returned from Dallas. It always was.

I carefully poured water into the Keurig, one of the many delightful treats Leah brought from her condo, and munched absently on a pretzel from the previous night's snackfest. It got me thinking about Natalie…and Morgan. Now that was an odd pair. Neither of them had anything in common. Then again, what did I know? I'd been off-base about Natalie. Or, maybe Natalie was just off as of late?

And, what did I know about Morgan, other than what Charlie had told me, which was very little? How had she hooked up with Davis Conrad? And why was she on leave? It obviously wasn't to help Charlie with his defense. To my knowledge, she hadn't even gone to see him since his arrest. Who was Morgan Thompson?

I sipped my coffee, effectively burning my tongue on the first attempt as I called my friend, Stacy, at the bar association. We'd met while volunteering at an animal rescue festival in North Scottsdale years earlier and had been friends ever since. Not only was she a fierce animal advocate, she also had an inside line on the legal community. If anyone could get the goods on Morgan, it was Stacy.

Stacy knew about Charlie's arrest and after a brief explanation of what I needed, put me on hold. I assumed she was going to provide me with a number for another contact, but when she returned she gave me one better.

"As it turns out, Morgan is not exactly on a leave of absence. She's been suspended from the firm and her partnership placed under review for undisclosed disciplinary reasons. All of this went down…let's see…about three weeks ago. I would need to make a direct inquiry to get more specific details."

"Nah, hold off on that. Leah and I don't need to be raising any more red flags at this point. At least this tells us why she's not at her job. Now I need to find out more about her background here in Arizona."

Stacy snorted. "It shouldn't be too hard, given her family connections."

"I don't follow."

"Geez, AJ. I thought you knew. Morgan's the daughter of the former state senator, Davis Conrad." Wow, Nicoh could have knocked me over with his tail. Morgan Thompson was Morgan Conrad. I certainly hadn't seen that one coming.

After I thanked Stacy and promised to treat her to lunch for her assistance, I immediately typed Morgan's name into the search engine on my trusty laptop. Why hadn't I thought of doing this before? There was more information than I ever wanted to know about Charlie's ex-girlfriend and her family.

Morgan had gone to a boarding school on the east coast—the same one her socialite mother, Cecilia Thompson, had attended before marrying a young attorney named Davis Conrad. Shortly after her father became a state senator, during Morgan's junior year in high school, she changed her name—perhaps to avoid the scrutiny that often followed children of public figures? If so, why choose her mother's maiden name? Perhaps it was preferable to be known as the daughter of a renowned socialite than one of a politician with questionable integrity? Regardless of her rationale, by the time Morgan headed off to Harvard, she was known as Morgan Thompson.

From all appearances, Morgan had gotten into the Ivy League on her own accord, excelled while she was there and graduated with honors. Her post-Harvard years were equally successful. She was the youngest person to make partner in the prestigious San Francisco law firm and until recently, had a stellar record.

Many of the online photos depicted the Conrad family on happy occasions—social and political outings, family get-together, even several with their brood of Scottish Terriers, all named after past or present Supreme Court Justices. I was squinting at a few pictures taken of Morgan and another familiar face at Harvard when Leah shuffled into the kitchen, hair standing on end, eyes puffy from sleep and too many salt-rimmed margaritas.

"What's up?" she murmured sleepily, grabbing my coffee cup and taking a long swig as I swung the laptop around to face her.

"Morgan was Greg's girlfriend before she dated Charlie." I pointed at the beaming couple, taken during happier times during their college days.

Leah sat the mug down with a clunk and stared at the screen. "Wow, small world. How come we never knew about this?"

She seemed miffed that such a juicy detail would have slipped her radar. I shrugged and filled her in on Morgan's background—including her famous family and subsequent name swap—and worked my way to her current career-botching snafu.

"So, I guess we now know the senator's guest was legit," I commented as Leah nibbled her lip.

"Do we?" Leah replied absently. "Do we know it was legit? If so, how come Charlie didn't know? And why all the secrecy?"

"What if Morgan hadn't been his intended guest? Maybe Morgan decided to accompany her dad after the arrangement to disable the security camera had been made."

"Or because the arrangement was made."

"Exactly."

"I may have a way to get some more background on Morgan, to find out the reason behind her suspension." She drained the last of my coffee and retreated to her room.

I groaned, not only was I out of coffee, I didn't want to know how she was going to get that information. Not one single drop.

* * *

I half-expected Leah to be napping when I checked on her a couple of hours later, but as I wiggled a fresh cup of joe through the partially opened doorway, a snicker emerged before the mug was snatched and the door thrown open. Leah's face beamed as she did a victory dance, the mug's contents precariously sloshing from side to side.

"Spill it before you actually do. What did you learn?" A mass of notepads was strewn about every surface. It was how she worked best, though given her lack of organizational skills, I marveled at her ability keep it all straight. Most of the time, I was convinced the notepads served as impressive-looking props while she stored all the pertinent goodies in her head.

"Well…" She loved drawing out the suspense. Of course, considering my best friend was more impatient than a canine at dinner time, the tension-building was typically short-lived. This time was no different. "Turns out Morgan's strong suit is not creative accounting. She's facing disciplinary sanctions—including disbarment and prosecution—for unauthorized utilization of the firm's funds."

"What the heck does that mean? Is that legalese for she embezzled from her firm?"

"Technically, she did use the funds without permission, but it was for a good cause." She bobbed her head in an attempt to convince me.

I wasn't buying—besides, when had she become such an advocate of Morgan's? Wasn't Charlie our priority? We certainly didn't have time to worry about Morgan's indiscretions and said as much.

"A good cause as in what—a big sale at Barney's?"

Leah chuckled. "That's what I thought, too. Turns out, Morgan possesses a quality her Harvard pals Charlie and Parker, not to mention that father of hers, don't. Loyalty. Especially where her mother is concerned."

"Senator Conrad's wife, Cecilia?"

Leah nodded. "She's been missing from the social scene for a while now, shortly after her husband's term ended. Apparently, she's been battling Huntington's—the Thompson family carries the gene."

I gasped. I didn't know much about it, but from what I'd heard, Huntington's was a cruel disease that wasted away nerve cells in the brain, causing rampant devastation to one's mind and body. Among the casualties were severely affected muscle and motor skills, along with dementia. Presently, there was also no known cure.

"She's currently in a private facility, the same one that cared for her sister, Morgan's aunt, until her death. Apparently, she'd had a long, excruciating battle with the same disease, which brings me to the reason behind Morgan's suspension." She paused to catch her breath. "From what I understand, the facility has been struggling to keep its head above water for a while now, like everyone during this economic downturn. The principals also made some unfortunate business decisions along the way and now they're faced with closing several facilities, including the one where Morgan's mother resides.

"Of course, the family can certainly afford to move her else-where, but think about the disruption, not to mention stress, it would cause her. And let's not forget about the other residents, many of whom are without the means to go elsewhere.

"Apparently, Morgan went to her father for assistance, but he refused to intervene because of the perception it would put out into the political universe. Favoritism…crap excuses like that."

I groaned. "Let me guess, Morgan took money from her law firm to keep her mother's facility in the black."

Leah nodded. "Just enough to keep things going, in small enough amounts to fly under the radar."

"How long did this go on?"

"Two years, give or take." Talk about modern day Robin Hood. Morgan certainly hadn't seemed suited for the role. "Any-way, her borrowing finally caught up with her. Or rather, her firm caught on. My source did intimate at least a couple of the other partners had been aware of Morgan's actions all along."

"Perhaps hoping she would put it back?"

"Yeah, something like that. Regardless, what Morgan did was

criminal. Her firm's desire to minimize the fallout is the main reason she's not in jail yet."

I laughed, though I wasn't feeling jovial. "I'm sure Senator Conrad feels the same way."

"That would be an affirmative."

"Where did you get this information, anyway?"

"You don't want to know."

"The rational side of me says no, but the other side that enjoys the sick fascination of knowing how you do the devious things you do? She's winning out."

"Ok, you asked, but don't say I didn't warn you," she teased as I pretended to cover my ears. "I found some juicy tidbits using the pictures you scrounged up on the Internet." She laughed at my doubtful glance. "Seriously, I jotted down the names of the people in the pictures with Morgan and created a roster of sorts. Turns out, she still keeps in touch with a couple of her law school buddies. One of them happens to work at the same law firm. In fact, he was grateful to Morgan because she helped bring him on board."

"And just like that"—I snapped my fingers—"he gave up dirt on Morgan?"

"He did…" she replied slowly, "after I told him in addition to the possible disbarment and prosecution she faced as a result of her issues with the firm, Morgan was also being looked at as an accessory in the murder of one of her childhood chums. One who also happened to be an alum."

I chuckled. "You are brutal—creative—but brutal."

Leah gave me her best evil genius laugh. "You'd be surprised what a guy would do to save a fair maiden."

"Oh yeah, totally getting that whole damsel in distress vibe off Morgan," I replied sarcastically, thinking of the conversation we'd recently had with her. She'd more likely reward the chivalry by shoving hot pokers into his eyes.

It did make me wonder about the dynamic between Morgan, Parker and Charlie once Greg had passed. To date, no one had been forthcoming about the nature of their relationships with one another and frankly, I was fed up with all the secrecy.

"Do me a favor?" Leah looked at me sideways, but nodded. "Keep an eye on Nicoh and Pandora. There's something I need to do," I looked at my watch, "sooner rather than later."

"Where are you going?" she asked.

"To have a little chat with Charlie. Before we go any further with this wild goose chase, I want to know exactly where we stand."

At this point, I wasn't sure of anything, other than there was a distinct possibility we'd been running around like chickens this whole time, while the murderer sat in jail.

CHAPTER SEVENTEEN

Charlie was even more pale this visit. Like vampire pale. It didn't occur to me until much later that it was due to his missed spray tan appointments. His demeanor was more upbeat on this visit, given that his minions were out there working hard to get him out of his current predicament. *Always someone there to clean up your mess for you, isn't there?* I grumbled, fully prepared to wipe the smile off his face. I figured there were only a couple of ways the conversation could go: A, Charlie would give me the information I wanted and I would return to being a good little minion or B, he'd continue to hold out on pertinent information, I'd punch him in the throat and we'd end up sharing a cell. I preferred option A, but was warming up to B.

"You have something?" his voice was hopeful as he searched my face.

"Leah and I have been doing some…research," I worked to keep both my tone and expression blank, "though honestly, we aren't exactly sure what we have, other than a crock filled with half-truths." Charlie's eyes widened. "You failed to mention that Morgan dated Greg first." Correct that—his eyes popped. He hadn't expected me to confront him. I waited expectantly for him to compose his thoughts.

"That was…a long time ago," he replied after a moment. "You know what happened."

"I know Greg died. They were together then?"

He nodded. "They dated off and on in high school and throughout college."

"So, they were obviously serious."

"Sure, as serious as Morgan gets."

"Well, golly gee, Charlie. She strikes me as someone who is as serious as say…murder." He balked. It was cruel but at least I had his attention. "You also knew about her mother's illness."

"She was diagnosed while we were dating. It wasn't the reason we stopped seeing each other, though."

"Do I want to know?"

"Morgan's always been a bit…intense, even when we were at Harvard."

"What about in high school? I was surprised I never knew her, much less knew she was the senator's daughter."

"The three of us knew her because of our parents. It was a society thing." He shrugged. "No reason you would have known her."

"Nice, Charlie, truly appreciate the condescending dig."

"I didn't mean it like that. You're just being difficult, you know what I meant."

"Getting back to Morgan—you mentioned her being intense. So you wouldn't be surprised if I told you she was currently suspended and facing possible disbarment." I quickly filled him in on Morgan's creative use of the firm's resources. I'm not sure what reaction I expected but Charlie's expression remained neutral as he eyed me silently. I decided to take a pass on that for the time-being. I had other ground to cover.

"Why did you dismantle the video before the party?"

He held my gaze for a moment before looking away. "It was at the senator's request."

I gestured for him elaborate and when he didn't respond immediately, I filled in the blanks. "He had a special guest that he was bringing to the party—one that would be present but not to be seen accompanying him."

Charlie's mouth dropped open. "How did you know?"

"Leah and I watched the videos, Charlie. We saw you in the parking garage before you dismantled the cameras and after, during your conversation with Arch."

"I don't understand. If you knew, they why did you..." His jaw clenched. "You wanted to see if I would lie." He sighed when I didn't respond, his pale, cracked lips pursing, "Senator Conrad likes to bring a friend with him. It wasn't the first time I've had to accommodate such a request." The way he said it led me to believe the former senator wasn't the only guest of Charlie's trying to conceal extracurricular activities.

"You ever know who the friends were?"

He shook his head. "It would be hard to tell. Many of my guests bring a plus one. And frankly, I don't care. It's good business." I assumed he meant having someone like David Conrad in his corner and wondered if it had been worth it.

"So, on the night of the party, it's safe to say you weren't aware which partygoer had accompanied the senator?"

"No idea."

"Would you be surprised to learn it was Morgan?"

"Right, he went to all that trouble so he could bring his daughter to the party." He frowned when I nodded. "That makes no sense—why would she sneak in—she already had an invite."

"I have no idea. You previously indicated she and Natalie weren't friends—what about Natalie and Arch, were they friendly?"

Charlie snorted. "No, definitely not."

"What do you know about Arch?"

"What kind of question is that? He's my assistant—it's not like he would have…hurt Parker…" I looked at him impatiently. He raised his hands in defeat, "Ok, ok…just answer the question." He blew out a long breath. "Honestly, not much. He lives in Mesa now. I think he used to live with his mom until she died a while back. I got the impression she'd been sick for some time, though I'm not familiar with the details. He never talked about it, but I overheard him talking to the hospice toward the end. `

"Then, when he came back to work for me, he told me he'd moved. Place must have been a dump in a pretty seedy area, because he constantly worried about going home, finding the place broken into and his belongings either gone or destroyed." He shook his head, disgusted, "I don't know how people can live like that."

"Not everyone is born with money, Charlie." He started to protest, but I stopped him, "Why did you rehire him, anyway?"

He grumbled. "Considering he's taken up residence in my absence—and hasn't bothered to visit once—I'm seriously starting to wonder the same thing. It was Natalie's idea. She made a pretty good case using that second chance nonsense. She can be surprisingly convincing when she wants to." Somehow, I didn't doubt that in the least.

The guard entered and told us our time was up. As he collected Charlie, I threw out on last question, "On the day of the White Party, where did you go from 12:30 to 6:40 p.m. while the rest of us were setting up?" Surely he couldn't deny it this time, knowing Leah and I had seen the video?

His eyes flashed with anger, surprising me. "Stay out of it, AJ. It has nothing to do with this, or with you." He turned on his heel and nodded to the guard, leaving me to stare at his back. As he marched through the doorway, he hesitated for a moment. "Not everyone deserves second chances."

* * *

As if my conversation with Charlie hadn't been enough of a treat, I had another one waiting when I exited the police station. I was brooding and would have normally missed her had it not been for her combative stance as she leaned against her Audi, arms crossed and foot tapping, irritation rippling from her like whitecaps. All six feet of her curvaceous figure were clad in black, from studded biker jacket to skin-hugging jeans to the knee-high riding boots with fierce-looking toeplates. Even her hair whipped angrily as the wind picked up, as if sensing a storm was brewing. If she'd been going for effect, it worked. Startled, I tripped over my size nine Chuck Taylors, barely catching myself before tumbling nose first into the sidewalk. If my reaction had amused her in the least, it failed to translate to her expression.

"The famous Arianna Jackson," Morgan's voice was husky as she slid aviators to the tip of her nose, her perusal overtly disapproving. "You're here visiting Charlie, I presume?" I didn't respond, more preoccupied with maintaining a safe distance.

"Don't bother answering that. I know you and your little blond-haired friend have been running around town asking questions, hoping to clear his good name. Well, even smart girls need some advice from time to time." Before I could reply, she cut the space between us until I could smell the combination of her musky perfume and cinnamony breath.

"Things are not always as they seem, Arianna. Sometimes it's better to leave them alone than it is to involve yourself in something you don't understand." I may have been mistaken, but it sounded more like a threat than friendly advice. Morgan stared at me, her eyes boring into mine and for a moment, I thought she would elaborate. Instead, she unceremoniously pushed her sunglasses up, turned on her heel and strode back to her car.

She was at the driver's door before I finally spoke, "And what about the truth, Morgan? Are we to leave it alone, too?" She paused just long enough I was convinced she would return to infringe upon my personal space.

She remained in place, though her mouth quirked. "I guess that depends upon whose truth you seek." She started to get into her Audi, effectively dismissing me.

I thumbed behind me. "It's about his truth. And Parker's. Don't you think they deserve that?"

Her lips curled into a snarl. "Deserve? Parker is a little beyond deserving anything. The truth is for the living, Arianna. And honestly, even if it revealed itself, I doubt you'd like the outcome." This time, she got in, revved the engine and left me standing there, sucking her fumes.

* * *

I returned home to find Leah sitting in the kitchen, pouring over her laptop while scribbling frantically on a notepad. Nicoh bounded to me with Pandora following close behind, tails wagging expectantly. I chuckled and scratched them both until Leah came up for air.

"Well, that's interesting," she replied after I finished filled her in on my latest conversation with Charlie, as well as the surprise appearance from Morgan. "What do you make of her advice?"

"Not sure. I wonder how she knew I would be there in the first place."

Leah shrugged. "Same way I know what I know." Right… inside information. One of these days, I'd need to expand my own network of confidential informants. I added it to my mental checklist, right after "get Charlie out of jail" and "find Parker's killer."

"I'm not saying your chats with Charlie and Morgan weren't enlightening, but do you wanna hear what I've got?" I sighed, but nodded. "Against my better judgment, I talked to Vargas…dum, dum, dum. Charlie's not the only one without a decent alibi for the time of Parker's murder."

"Mystery witness, notwithstanding."

"Right, right…but except for that witness, Arch, Morgan, Natalie and at least a dozen people were either at home alone or with someone who couldn't be forced to incriminate them. Meaning, we've got a whole list of people, other than Charlie, who had the opportunity to kill Parker and dump him afterward."

"Ok, that gives us other people with opportunity, big whoopee. Sorry, but that isn't a showstopper, Leah. The police already have that list and Charlie's still behind bars." I didn't want diminish her efforts, but that tidbit by itself got us nowhere. We needed less gristle and more meat. "What about motive?"

"Bear with me here. Some of the things Charlie told you meshed with what I just found out—for starters, Arch's mom."

"Charlie said she passed away. What does she have to do with this?"

"Well, I reached out into the information highway and found some juicy stuff on Senator Conrad's family—his wife, Cecilia, to be specific. Remember the sister with Huntington's?"

I snapped my fingers. "Right, the one that was in the same facility as Mrs. Conrad."

"That's the one. Before Arch's mom was Marie Underwood, she was Marie Thompson."

I blew out a low whistle. "Cecilia Conrad's sister. Morgan and Arch are cousins." Another puzzle piece found its way home.

Leah gave me a small, satisfied smile. "Hang on, Rockfish, I'm not done yet. When we met at Los Olivos, Natalie had come from volunteering at a long term care facility. She mentioned the funding she'd been working to obtain had finally come through."

"It's same facility where Mr. Thompson currently resides? So

Natalie knows Morgan's mother…and possibly knew Arch's as well?"

She nodded. "Likely, it's a small facility and Natalie's been volunteering there for years."

"Interesting, but other than providing a connection between Morgan, Natalie and Arch, it doesn't seem particularly…devious."

"Maybe not, but when you combine it with Natalie's bizarre behavior, her meeting with Arch and now Morgan's not-so-subtle threat, it means something."

I snorted. "Yeah, it mean three people who also know Charlie and Parker are all either related or connected in some way. It still doesn't scream motive for murder."

"Are you playing devil's advocate now, or just trying to be a buzz kill?" Leah was clearly incensed by my blasé attitude toward her research efforts.

"I'm not insinuating they're all coincidences, but we need something more concrete than the evidence the police currently have, including the witness who puts Charlie near the parking garage at the time of Parker's murder."

"Ugh, I knew I forgot to ask Vargas something. You mind?" I shook my head as she whipped out her cell phone and dialed. When Vargas answered, she put him on speakerphone.

"Hey Detective, Leah and AJ here, you have a few seconds for a couple of your favorite citizens?"

Vargas groaned. "Didn't I just talk to you? I do work, you know. Speaking of which, it would make my job a whole lot easier if a particular couple of Nancy Drew wannabes stopped mucking up the works on the Parker Harris case."

"First off," Leah retorted playfully, "we're more along the lines of Charlie's Angels—Charlie being, well Charlie, with me as Jill and AJ as Kelly." We heard Vargas snort on the other end of the connection. "Second, it isn't our job to make your job easier. It's our job to make sure you're *doing* your job, giving Charlie a fair shake, that type of thing. So for now, we'll let that whole mucking reference slide—if you agree to help us."

Vargas snorted. "Well, just so that we're clear. I'm not playing Bosley in this little fantasy. The two of you are going to get me into hot water for all the tips I've provided to your little side investigation."

"Hey, you'd better keep my good name out of that. Leah's been the one doing all the cajoling. I'm just an innocent bystander," I teased.

"That's not what I hear. The two of you—yes, I said two—are notorious for getting yourselves into all kinds of situations where you shouldn't have been sticking your noses in the first place." We both started to protest, but Vargas intervened. "So, getting back to the reason you called."

"Right, right, we know you've gone through the videos for the days surrounding the murder. What if we told you we'd been given access to the feed from the security cameras *inside* Charlie's penthouse and there were a few juicy morsels that would not only help your case, but might change your perspective on the murderer?"

Leah's query was met with silence. "Detective, you still with us?"

A grumble came from the other end of the extension. "I'm here. I'm just trying to decide whether I should go over there and arrest you both for obstruction. In case you two Nancy—err, Charlie's Angels weren't aware, it is a crime to withhold evidence pertinent to an ongoing investigation."

"Uh, consider what we've told you a peace offering?" I feebly countered.

Another grumble, or maybe it was a growl. "I'll get back to you on that. Meanwhile, I'll be there in ten. Do I need to tell you two to stay put?" He hung up before we could respond and fortunately, before I had the opportunity to tell him I'd never figured him for a Bosley type, anyway.

* * *

"Good going, *Jill*…you could have at least warned me you were going to give up the goods. And, you didn't even get the scoop on the witness, which was the purpose of the call." I threw my hands up, actually kind of scared that Vargas would arrive in… oh, nine minutes and counting now…with two pairs of handcuffs in tow. Leah nodded silently, having arrived at a similar conclusion.

When the doorbell rang in what seemed less than the ten minutes Vargas had threatened, I hoped Leah had concocted a solution in that spiky little head of hers. I contemplated hiding out, but Nicoh and Pandora made enough noise to let the detective know we were home. Sucking in a deep breath, I opened the door to an intense-looking Detective Vargas. To my surprise, he had brought backup.

Ramirez.

Undeterred, Leah cawed over my shoulder, "Oooh, Starsky and Hutch ride again. Since when does PPD tag along with TPD, anyway? You need special reinforcement on this one, Detective Vargas?" And there she went, dashing all hope we'd be able to talk our way out of this predicament.

"When TPD's poker game is interrupted by meddling busy-bodies," Vargas snapped, stepping through the doorway as Ramirez followed, his stature equally imposing and expression consumed with barely-contained fury.

He caught me by surprise when he whispered in my ear as he passed, "He was losing anyway."

I started to laugh but he put a finger to my lips and shook his head before leveling me with look that catapulted a series of chills down my spine and clearly communicated Leah and I wouldn't be getting off that easily.

"So, we're here to pick up those videos," Vargas' tone was all business as he glanced around.

"Well, had you not ended the conversation so abruptly, we could have saved you a trip and your poker game," Leah replied tersely, though Vargas looked unconvinced. "You access these videos through Internet links…you know…using a computer?"

"I know how to use a computer, Leah," Vargas snapped impatiently. "Let's see 'em." He gestured to the laptop she had left on the kitchen island, though his eyes were focused on the array of snacks still strewn about from the previous night. "Did we interrupt something?"

Leah blushed. "Natalie Ingram stopped by last night to share some information she had gotten about the investigation—inside information." She glanced warily at Vargas.

"Well, she certainly didn't get anything from me," he replied sharply. "I'm a one girl per investigation type of source."

Despite being furious, he managed to slip her a smoldering look before his brusque demeanor returned. It was my turn to blush and look away while Leah ignored him, pretending to focus on her laptop. Once she accessed the correct feed, she fast-forwarded to the interaction between Arch and Natalie before swiveling the laptop toward the detectives.

Though his irritation was just as palpable as Vargas', Ramirez had been surprisingly quiet to this point. "Interesting that Wilson never mentioned these cameras," he commented once they finished watching the feed, before turning his steely gaze on us.

Though I personally wanted to squirm my way out of the room, beyond the reach of its intensity, both Leah and I responded with tiny shrugs. Who knew why Charlie did half the things he did, or didn't do. Maybe he hadn't been sure what they'd find. One thing was certain, throughout the course of the investigation he hadn't gone out of his way to make things easier for the police, much less for himself.

I still wondered where he'd been all those hours prior to the party and why he was overtly evasive, if not hostile, when I'd brought it up. A bit too late, I realized I'd muttered that last bit out loud. Leah could only shake her head while both detectives stared at me. Vargas' gaze was a bit more scrutinizing than I liked, his midnight-colored eyes drilling into mine. I bit my lip, seriously hoping handcuffs and a ride in a smelly police cruiser weren't in my immediate future.

Fortunately, he glanced away. "We plan on finding out. Wilson contends he had several private business meetings that afternoon but up to this point, has refused to divulge who they were with. We know it wasn't Harris. We've located and interviewed the individuals he'd been with during that time and Wilson was not among those present."

I nodded. "Speaking of being present, the witness who placed Charlie at the parking garage, does she happen to live in his building?"

Vargas squinted. "It's funny you should ask. Off the record, no, she wasn't a resident, nor did she live at the address she provided. No one with that name did. We're still trying to track her down, but it appears she's in the wind."

I looked at Leah. We'd caught a break. The only witness placing Charlie at the scene had gone missing, or perhaps she'd never existed. Either way, the County Attorney's case was starting to crack. A few more whacks and maybe, just maybe, Leah and I would be able to break this nut wide open…meaning the two of us could turn out to be Charlie's angels. Stranger things have happened. Right?

CHAPTER EIGHTEEN

"We barely dodged a bullet with those two," Leah commented, a long moment passing as the detectives descended the steps. It felt like a staircase scene from a Hitchcock movie—long and agonizing.

"Yeah, but we learned the witness was bogus."

"True—" She was interrupted by the doorbell.

We looked at each other in horror. Surely the detective hadn't changed their minds about hauling us off in handcuffs? As we stood there silently debating about what to do, it rang again. And again. Pandora surprised us when she rushed toward it, barking and dancing on her hind legs. Considering the detectives would not have elicited that reaction, I motioned for Leah to open the door. Pandora's dad, Randy, stood there, a confused look on his face as he glanced over his shoulder.

"Was that…the police I saw leaving?"

"Um, yeah, they're friends of ours." Randy nodded skeptically.

Leah ushered him in, while I bolted out a bit too enthusiastically, "You're home early!"

He flushed, shifting from one foot to the other while tapping his cell phone against his thigh. "Err…about that. It turns out… I'm moving."

"Oh, wow. Like to Ahwatukee or something?" Leah asked.

"Err…no," Randy replied quietly, lowering his eyes, "to Dallas. The client I've been working with needs a bit more hand-holding than was originally thought. My firm has assigned me to oversee their account, indefinitely." He shrugged. "Essentially, that could mean three years or it could translate to something longer. I'll still keep the house here until we figure things out, but in the interim, they've set me up in a condo." He babbled, clearly excited about the new opportunity, but he'd lost me back at the whole "moving" part.

"So, you'd like for me to keep Pandora while you are out there?" I asked once he finished. Leah nodded, absently scratching both dogs while their tails beat against her legs.

"What? Oh no, I could never ask you to do that. I actually came back to get her and to pack a few necessities. I've got to head back by the end of the weekend—start the week fresh and all."

Randy searched our faces, hoping for approval. I hadn't had a chance to digest his news, so I wasn't sure what vibe I was giving him. Pandora wasn't mine, so I certainly couldn't say no. I looked into Nicoh's eyes, so brown and soft, his current happy expression and waggy tail. I knew losing his best gal pal would be tough. Pandora hadn't left his side and—sensing something was amiss—nudged the base of his ear with her muzzle, her own tail fluttering in short sporadic beats. I exhaled a deep breath, praying I could keep the waterworks at bay, at least until Randy departed.

"Congratulations, Randy. I mean that. We'll certainly miss you…both. I know Nicoh will miss his pal. Would you be able to bring her by before you leave on Sunday?"

He nodded and scruffed Nicoh under the chin. "Definitely. I

know it will be an adjustment for Ms. P., too, but we'll return every other month or so, so we'll be back before you know it."

I gave them both quick, fierce hugs and managed to see them out before a single tear broke free. Nicoh howled sadly. Leaning against the closed door, I let out a long breath and looked at Leah, who had been uncharacteristically quiet during Randy's visit. Her eyes were rimmed in red, mouth pursed as she too, fought the inevitable downpour.

* * *

My emotions were shot and brain mush as my body needled me with fatigue. I needed to keep moving—even if it was mindless busywork. After some less than stellar housecleaning, I mulled over my latest project, photographing a series of galleries that were part of the seasonal downtown art walk. The city's Chamber of Commerce was my client—and while the turnaround time was short—the paycheck was substantial and much-needed.

Unfortunately, my mind wandered as I read the specs. First, to the loved ones I'd lost and then to the ones I'd lost but never known. Though it had been no fault of my own, their absence still stung. In fact, it weighed on me more than I'd ever confess. Immediate on my mind were my two sets of parents—the first had raised me and the second had given me life—and my sister. I had never gotten the opportunity to meet the latter three and was left with a hole where they should have been and where so many questions remained unanswered. Leah and Nicoh were my family now, as were my close circle of friends—Ramirez, the Stanton brothers—even Charlie. If I'd learned anything over the past few years, most of us would protect the ones we cared for at any cost.

That's when it clicked. To this point, the police had assumed Parker had been murdered because of a bad business deal, that the motive had been simple greed. What if they were wrong? What if the reason had been more deeply rooted. Deeper than revenge or retribution? What if the choices Parker made had put him on a path, one that sealed his destiny? In making those choices, Parker had crossed a line that changed lives, divided families. Would that be enough reason to kill? If there was one thing I could be sure of —when it came to Parker Harris—you'd better believe it.

Grimacing, I placed the call, nibbling on a fingernail as I counted rings, convinced I would end up with voicemail.

"What do you want now, Jackson?" Vargas growled, picking up after five.

"It's nice to talk to you again too, Detective,"

"Whatever. What do you want? Keep in mind I'm trying to run an investigation here. So, unless you have more information, this isn't a two-way street. As it is, I'm sitting here—on my night off—watching video footage I received at the thirteenth hour."

"Actually, it's not even midnight yet." I tried my best to be helpful.

"You know, you two are lucky I didn't arrest you for with-holding evidence." Hadn't we already covered this ground? I decided not to stir that pot, the big guy wasn't in the best of moods. "I'm not sure the term 'thin ice' has any meaning to you." Vargas exhaled.

"I'm sorry, Detective. I'll preface this by saying I would like to avoid a private escort to the police station in your cruiser, but I do have a question."

He scoffed. "Ramirez warned me you were a pill." Ramirez had called me a pill? Truth be told, I hadn't previously been fond of the spitfire reference, but this took things to another level. At some point in the immediate future, Ramirez and I would need to have a little chat. "I don't have all day, Action Jackson."

"Err, yeah…sorry, got distracted. I'm curious about the missing witness. Did you talk to her personally?"

"No, she approached one of the patrolmen the day we pulled Harris from Tempe Town Lake. He was working the scene perimeter, manning the crowd, when she just showed up."

"So he has a description?"

"A rough one. It was crazy down there that day. Always is when we pull one out, draws the lookie loos like overfed pigeons." I heard papers shuffling. "Here it is. Margaret O'Connor. Late twenties to early thirties. Tall, between 5 feet 11 inches and 6 feet 1 inch. Wearing a black windbreaker, tennis shoes and black baseball cap that covered the majority of her hair, which he thought might have been reddish-brown. No description of her features. Apparently she was wearing sunglasses that covered the better part of her face. That's about it."

"What about the dog?"

"Yeah, what about it?"

"What did it look like?"

"Officer said it was small and black with pointy ears. Not being a dog person he wasn't sure about the breed." He paused to laugh. "He did note it was the type you'd expect to see wearing a red plaid sweater. It wasn't…wearing a sweater, that is, red or otherwise. Oh, and he heard her call it Ginsburg—odd name for a dog."

I shook my head, not odd at all. O'Connor and Ginsburg were both names of Supreme Court Justices.

Vargas knew I was on to something, but before he could threaten the handcuffs again, I feigned sleepiness and ended the conversation. For the next several minutes, I sat alone in the dark and thought, continuing to torture that fingernail in the process.

I went back to the beginning and thought about Charlie. And Parker. And Greg. I added Natalie, Morgan and Arch into the mix.

Six people.

Two were dead.

One by suicide.

One by murder.

One was in jail.

Three remained.

Linked by blood or by circumstance, all three had been less than truthful as of late. Whether it had been by omission or outright lie had no bearing. Each had guilty knowledge and more importantly, means, motive and opportunity. In the end all the deception, mistruths and subterfuge led to the same destination and the same conclusion.

One of them had murdered Parker.

CHAPTER NINETEEN

In hindsight, I suppose I should have called Vargas back, or Ramirez, at a minimum. I'd been warned by both about my continued involvement, yet even the threat of jail couldn't sway me. Unfortunately, selective listening wasn't my only flaw. I'd also inherited stubbornness from my parents. I hoped it wouldn't prove fatal.

I shook my head, time was running out and Charlie was about to be formally charged with murder. I had to trust my gut and forge ahead, no matter how harebrained my scheme might have been.

I wanted to tell Leah my plan, but when I snuck a peek into her room, only tufts of hair were visible from beneath the covers. Instead, I left her snoozing, justifying it as much-needed rest. Nicoh, too, was crashed, his large frame sprawled across the bed, head buried beneath a mass of pillows. My decision made, I left Leah a detailed note, glanced around and pulled the door shut, hoping I'd come back in one piece.

I cursed after finding the Mini low on gas and borrowed Leah's SUV, knowing she'd already be grumpy about missing out on the adventure. I made a mental note to pick up Starbucks on the way home as a peace offering and after glancing at the clock, hoped it would be open by the time I made my return trip.

Had I not been so engrossed in thought, I would have noticed the car following a good measure behind, especially considering I'd been through this scenario before. Given my past experiences, you'd think a girl would learn.

Traffic was limited, so I made good time across the cities and was pleased to find I had my choice of parking on the barren Tempe streets. Stu buzzed me in without question and after a brief conversation, I proceeded to the penthouse. I had checked the video feed before I'd left and while I had not seen him, I knew Arch was in there somewhere. It was dark when I entered, not surprising considering the hour, though I half-expected him to be playing The Legend of Zelda on Charlie's Wii while eating Doritos or some other greasy, color-injected snack on the pristine leather couches. My only guide through the space was the moon trickling through the skylights, causing me to narrowly miss a lamp as I shuffled along the walls. Someone had been moving things around in their boss' absence, I mused.

"What are you doing here?" Arch's voice came from the direction of the living room. After squinting for a moment, I was able to make out his silhouette, sitting alone in the darkness.

"I came to see you, of course." I chuckled in an effort to lighten the mood.

"No pet this time?" I couldn't see his face but his tone was glib.

My fingers found a light switch. Arch blinked even though the lighting was dim, indicating he'd been sitting like that for a while. He'd likely not slept recently either, as evidenced by his blood-shot eyes. Oddly enough, they defied an otherwise unruffled appearance. His hair was styled, face cleanly shaven and attire crisp. Had it not been for the circumstances, he looked ready to work or perhaps, to meet someone.

"You look tired, Arch. Not been sleeping well?" He shrugged and took a long drink from the cocktail glass he'd been clutching, draining the amber liquid until only ice cubes tinkled. As he placed it on the coffee table, I noticed the empty Maker's Mark bottle on its side.

"Hmm, guilty conscience, perhaps?"

His head snapped in my direction, though he averted his gaze. "My conscience is clear," he rasped.

I put my hands up in mock surrender. "Since I'm already here, care if I ask you a couple of questions then? He waved, indicating he didn't. "On the day of the White Party, what did you give Natalie?"

He squinted, his eyes meeting mine. "How did you know about that?" It was my turn to shrug and after scrutinizing me for a moment, he laughed. "Let me guess. Charlie's got this place geared up too," He shook his head, clearly not amused by the knowledge his boss had been keeping tabs on him.

"The key to Big Bess," he replied after a long pause.

I nodded. "Anything else?"

He chuckled. "Charlie's key card."

"Why did she say she wanted them?"

"Parker knew a friend of this classic car guy from California Charlie had talked about. Apparently he has his own show on the Speed channel?" I shook my head. I had no idea who or what he was referencing. "Anyway, Parker found out the car guy was going to be in town and thought it would be a hoot to have him detail Charlie's Eldorado. They needed the car keys to facilitate the surprise. She wanted the key card so that she could return the car keys in case I wasn't around when the guy finished." Was he serious?

"I'm not buying it, Arch. Even if that story was true, either Parker or Natalie could have returned the car keys while you were here. The party was that night. It wasn't like you were going anywhere before then. They certainly didn't need Charlie's key card for that."

"It was what she wanted. She didn't want to spoil the surprise if something didn't work out as planned." I'll bet she didn't.

"But you gave her more than those two items, didn't you? You gave her Charlie's code to parking garage as well." Though he tried to mask his surprise, his eye twitched.

"Why?" I pressed. This time he shrugged but didn't respond. "Ok, so when the police determined Parker had been killed that same day, in the parking garage, with the car whose keys you'd just handed off…that didn't seem suspect to you?"

"Natalie didn't have anything to do with that. It's just a coincidence."

"Right, a coincidence Charlie supposedly killed Parker using Big Bess, while Natalie was in possession of the only set of keys? 'Cause you can't be sure she ever returned them, can you?" I replied sarcastically. "Yeah, I'd say that was a real coincidence."

"I'm sure she had returned everything by then." The way he was defending her made me wonder if Arch had a thing for Natalie. After seeing how she'd treated him on the video, it was clear Arch didn't know much about women. "The police found them when they searched the penthouse, before they arrested Charlie." I shook my head. Copies could have been made and the originals returned during the party. It still didn't explain Charlie's missing key card.

Frustrated I wasn't getting anywhere with him, I changed tactics, "Did Natalie convince you to ask Charlie for your job back?"

"Why would she? I needed a job and Charlie hadn't filled mine yet, so I figured it was worth a shot. He doesn't stay mad long and frankly, the reason he severed our working relationship in the first place was bogus."

"So you'd be surprised if I told you she went to Charlie on your behalf and suggested it?"

He shook his head from side to side. "She wouldn't do that. Charlie asked me to come back because he needed me." *Asked?* Someone was seriously delusional. "In fact, he still needs me." I rest my case.

"All right, what about your cousin—what was her beef with Parker?"

He snorted. "Morgan? Everyone and everything pisses her off." At least he hadn't tried to deny their connection, though I could tell he was trying to figure out how I'd made it.

A sudden, satisfied twitch at the corner of Arch's mouth, followed by the slight shift of his eyes told me we were no longer alone in the penthouse. Natalie and Morgan had come to join our late night party. Someone had been keeping tabs on me.

"What? No margaritas?" Natalie appeared to be feeling particularly snotty.

She was dressed similarly to Morgan, still clad in the black ensemble from our previous confrontation. Maybe she was only allotted one death-eater costume per capital crime? I was about to comment, but decided sarcasm would be wasted on this crowd, even though it chafed me both were having such good hair days. I was sure my ponytail stood at all angles and could have afforded to have a pitchfork run through it, while Natalie's golden mane trailed down her back in a tidy braid and Morgan's auburn tresses billowed like flames. The breeze flowing through the open skylights only enhanced the effect.

Distracted by my hair envy, I had failed to notice both were also wearing gloves, and in Morgan's right hand clutched an equally fierce-looking piece of hardware. What surprised me more than the gun itself was that it wasn't aimed in my direction. Given his open-mouthed expression, I ventured a guess that Arch had noticed as well.

"You have a big mouth, cuz. You know that, don't you?"

Arch's eyes went wide. "What? I didn't tell her anything she didn't already know, I promise."

Morgan ignored his pleas, turning her black eyes toward me. "Natalie was convinced she could sway you and your little blond friend to side with us on this…matter. She lost that particular bet." She glanced at Natalie and laughed. "Pay up, Nat." Natalie pursed her lips in response.

"Side? What side is that?" I asked.

"Our side. Or Charlie's. I'm sorry to have to inform you that you picked the losing team, Arianna," Morgan's voice was husky.

"Why, because you have a gun?" My comment drew several annoyed glances.

"No, you simp. Because it's the right thing—the moral thing—to choose."

"Says the person holding the gun," I replied dryly.

Morgan threw her head back and laughed. "You are a feisty one. I'll give you that. No wonder Charlie keeps you around. You should take notes, Arch." Ignoring his seething looks, she turned back to me. "I'm guessing you want to know what's going on, which is why you chose the weakest link here." She wiggled the gun at Arch.

I nodded, no sense denying it now. Morgan lowered the gun and tapped it against her leg, while Natalie leaned against the wall, looking bored. Arch folded his arms and avoided looking at either of them, clearly enraged by his cousin's condescending jabs.

It was Natalie who spoke after a prolonged silence, "Parker and Charlie killed my brother. They killed Greg." Even Morgan stilled at the mention of his name.

"I thought Greg…committed suicide," I replied as quietly and gently as I could muster, but Morgan's head snapped in my direction, her eyes flashing.

"Because of Parker and Charlie…what they did to him…what they forced him to do."

Whatever had been stirring in Arch erupted as he launched himself at his cousin and slapped her hard across the face.

"Your precious Greg doesn't deserve your pity, you stupid cow! He was no better than they were. All three of them… killed…my mother, your aunt. It was their fault she died." Arch flopped into his chair while Morgan glared at him, a blotchy handprint forming on her face.

I thought she might be contemplating the advantages of shooting him, so I cleared my throat and attempted to diffuse the tension, "I'm sorry for your loss, I understand your mother had Huntington's before she passed?"

Arch nodded as he continued his stare down with Morgan. "She was in a private facility. Parker, Charlie *and* Greg were heavy into playing with the stock market—taking risks with other people's money—their usual modus operandi. She"—he dipped his head toward Morgan—"was dating Greg at the time and told him about a small group of investors representing various private healthcare facilities throughout the southwest. There's a large demand here for medical services due to the size and age of the population, as well as the type of transplants we attract from other states." I nodded, the term "snowbirds" popping into mind. "Greg took this information back to his cohorts, and they immediately concocted another money-making scheme the investors couldn't refuse. I mean, who would turn down the possibility of making millions, if not billions, within a relatively short time, if the risk was presented as being minimal?"

Morgan started to interject but Arch, with his renewed back-bone, cut her to the quick with a look. "I'm telling this part of the story, *cuz*." I noticed the rhythm of the gun tapping on her thigh had increased two-fold, but Morgan only nodded while Natalie looked on, her lips pressed into a tight line.

"As luck would have it…ha…what funny word. Luck." His laugh was harsh. "More like arrogance meets ignorance. Anyway, things went well, for a while. The boys made money. The investors made money. The facilities flourished. Everyone was happy. Until Parker got bored, as he inevitably would. He started dabbling on the side—the higher the risk, the better. It was all about living on the edge, being on the fringe. He was like an adrenaline junkie and money was his extreme sport. Only Parker wasn't playing with Monopoly money, or even his own. No, the real rush came from taking risks with *other* people's livelihood. And like any junkie, the high eventually wore off and when you're playing with real money, the consequences have devastating, life-altering affects. Investors couldn't honor their commitments. Their intended recipients were forced to either eliminate services and staff or close down entirely—leaving employees, patients, families and communities in peril. The facilities that were able to remain afloat did the best they could. And while I'm sure they would claim no one died as a result, patients were left to deteriorate without the benefit of services that would allow for appropriate diagnosis and treatment."

"People like your mother," I added, though Arch was lost in his thoughts and did not answer.

It was Morgan who responded, "She eventually died and of course, as Arch said, we couldn't prove it was because of the cutbacks. She was merely the result of her environment, they said, the victim of a ruthless disease. At the same time, my mother was already starting to show signs. We all will, someday." She stared out the window, her face unreadable.

I wondered what that must be like, to know your body was a ticking time bomb, and that one day you could wake up and not be…you? Regardless of what I thought about Morgan, no one deserved that.

"As Arch mentioned, I was dating Greg at the time," she gave

Natalie a sympathetic nod, the first compassionate gesture I'd seen her offer, "and despite what Arch *thinks*"—she shot him a less than endearing look—"Greg was devastated by Parker's actions—even pleading with Parker and Charlie, begging them to formulate a plan to replenish the funds—desperate to the point of utilizing his own money.

"Of course, Parker thought he was ridiculous and Charlie… well, by playing Switzerland, was essentially backing Parker, whether he would admit it to himself or not. The two of them went about doing what they always did when one game was over. They moved on to the next. In the meantime, Greg drove himself mad in his attempt to 'fix things,' as he would phrase it. It was just too much, too much devastation for one person to fix. 'Too much and too far gone,' he used to mumble near the end. Eventually, his conscience got the better of him…" her voice trailed off as she continued gazing out into the night.

Natalie's voice crackled, her throat dry, "He killed himself on the anniversary of Arch's mom's death." I withheld a gasp, I hadn't known that. "The three of them—Parker, Charlie and Greg —had only recently reconciled and in celebration, decided to road trip in Big Bess. The weather had been nice, so Charlie took the opportunity to get her out for a drive. I don't remember where they were ultimately headed, but their road trip took them into an area with mountainous, windy roads, hairpin turns and hair-raising drop-offs. At one point, they pulled off to look at the view. Parker and Charlie were joking back and forth about some nonsense and when they turned around, Greg launched himself over the guardrail using the tail end of Charlie's car. They tried to stop him but were too late. The last thing he said before he plunged to his death was 'Tell them I'm sorry…I tried to fix it, but it was just too far gone.'"

"I'm so sorry. I didn't know." No one had known the details surrounding Greg's suicide, which eerily mimicked that of my biological father, Martin. "I had a family member…pass…in a similar manner. I'm truly sorry."

Natalie nodded, her eyes glassy. "They retrieved his body eleven days later. It took them that long to…to get down to where he was." I nodded sadly. Martin's body had never been recovered. Never found. Honestly, I didn't know which would be worse. "Parker's actions not only ruined those facilities—indirectly or otherwise—he destroyed two families."

"So, all of this"—I waved my hand at the gun still tapping against Morgan's thigh—"is about revenge."

"Revenge?" Morgan seethed, her eyes piercing mine. "*This* is beyond revenge. Or retribution. *This* is about doing what's right."

"And two wrongs make a right in your book, I take." I replied flatly. "If that is the case, why punish Charlie?"

"'Why punish Charlie?' she asks," Morgan sneered. "I've given you way too much credit, Arianna. I didn't realize you were so ignorant to the ways of the world."

I shrugged, "Then educate me." The look I got in response told me not to toy with her. "I'm being serious, Morgan." She rolled her eyes, looking disgusted.

Instead, Natalie responded, "Charlie could have stopped Parker, yet he chose not to."

"So his inaction deemed him as culpable as Parker, and yielded him the same fate?" If Charlie got the death penalty, it essentially would be.

"Charlie *chose* his fate," Natalie clarified.

"It seems to me you've been manipulating things to suit your needs. And, if we're being completely honest here, that's not fate as much as it is—"

"Are you seriously trying to piss us off?" Morgan asked, incredulous that I would mess with a chick holding a loaded weapon.

I raised my hands in surrender. "Sorry, just trying to get some clarification. I'm still back at that 'beyond revenge or retribution' part of the conversation." I was rewarded with a slap upside the back of my head, compliments of the lovely Natalie. Not so girl-next-door after all.

"I warned you she had a smart mouth," Arch piped in. *Thanks, Arch,* I thought to myself. *I'll repay the favor by not telling you they're probably going to shoot you first.*

"Let's get a couple of things straight, shall we?" I noticed Morgan had repositioned the gun suspiciously close to my head. Perhaps I'd been hasty on my prior assessment? "From here on out, keep the commentary to yourself. Or you'll be eating jell-o through a straw." Though it could have been a good way to drop those M&M's binging pounds, it was probably not the time mention I preferred red raspberry jell-o over strawberry or cherry.

"Permission to ask you something, then?"

Natalie shook her head in annoyance, while Morgan looked amused by my gumption. "Charlie said you were a pain, but I had no idea." Considering Charlie annoys easily, I took that to be a compliment, as well as a thumbs-up to proceed.

"You dated Parker," I nodded at Natalie while Morgan scoffed. "Morgan, you dated Charlie. And you, Arch, work for him. Was all this an elaborate setup—an attempt to integrate your-selves into their world—to figure them out while learning their routines?"

Natalie clapped. "See Morgan, I told you she wasn't as dumb as she looks. Sorry AJ, but that hair?" She shot a finger pistol at my head—unnerving, to say the least. I made a note to have a chat with Paolo, my hair stylist, should I live to make it to my next appointment. "That and the company she keeps. Leah gives Kathy Griffin a run for her money in the talks-too-much cate-gory and is nowhere near as funny. If she didn't know so many people, I'd seriously consider dumping the broad. And that dog of yours, I'd ask the shelter you got him from for a refund. In the meantime, he could stand an air freshener and a breath mint."

It took everything in me not to throw her down and chop off the perky braid she was sporting. Insulting a girl's do was one thing, but insulting her best friend AND her dog pushed her right into WWE territory. Just as I channeled my inner John Cena with a Rock chaser, Natalie surprised me by responding.

"Getting back to your question—yes, the three of us became acquainted the day of my brother's funeral. Thanks for coming by the way. Greg always liked you. Despite the current circumstances, I can see why. You're a decent chick and unfortunately, loyal to a fault." I shrugged. It was what it was.

"Anyway, we installed Arch as Charlie's assistant. He was fresh out of college and needed a job, and as luck would have it, Charlie needed someone to help him oversee his day-to-day activities. He asked Parker for a referral and in turn, Parker asked me. Of course, I was happy to offer up Arch. Charlie never knew—and still doesn't—that he and Morgan are cousins."

"So the decision to kill Parker using Big Bess was because of Greg and the road trip?" Natalie nodded. It was sad that they chose to equate human life with an inanimate object, but Big Bess was the most important thing to Charlie and as they saw it, the best way to torture him.

"Arch, just to reconfirm, the day of the White Party you gave Charlie's car keys to Natalie, along with his penthouse key card and parking garage key code." When both Morgan and Natalie swiveled their heads toward him, I laughed. "Oh come on gals, we're way beyond establishing that. But how did you know Charlie would leave you alone long enough to facilitate the hand-off? You couldn't have known he would leave the penthouse that day, much less know when."

Arch shook his head. "I didn't. I certainly didn't expect him to leave during preparations for the White Party, but when he did, I called Natalie. She would have stopped by anyway, though this worked out to our advantage because we didn't have to concoct an excuse for her being there." I doubt this got him off the hook with Morgan and Natalie, who were both still looking at him with contempt.

"At some point, you gave the items to Morgan, didn't you, Natalie?" Both of them were noncommittal though given their body language, I could tell I was on the right track. "You arrived at the White Party first, with the former senator." I looked at Morgan, her face remained hard, unmoving. "Charlie wasn't aware you'd be your father's guest for the evening—he'd invited you separately and you'd accepted—so he had no way of knowing he'd be providing you with the access you needed to get in and out of the parking garage without being detected. So not only were the cameras disabled at the senator's request, you had both your father's and Charlie's key codes for the garage's entrance."

I shifted my attention to Natalie, who looked at me with an equally stony expression. "You…arrived before Parker, using your volunteer work at the hospital as an excuse to go to the party separately. I'm guessing this was because you need to ensure his car was still visible on the street the following day, another part of your ruse to make it appear as though he'd gone missing. Plus, you needed your own car so you and Morgan could get away cleanly after you dumped Parker into the lake.

"But something went wrong with the plan, didn't it?" I only had to look at one of them to know I'd hit a nerve. "As you were leaving the party, Parker unexpectedly called you a cab and rather than join you, he tucked you in and sent you on your merry way. You had to get to him before he left in his car and ruined everything, so you either called or texted Morgan, who was already lying in wait in the parking garage for you and Parker to arrive. And you"—I pointed at Morgan—"must have made up an excuse so your father would leave without you."

Morgan huffed, but replied, "Yes, Father and I left the party before Parker and Natalie, by design. Once in the garage, I told my father I had forgotten to tell Charlie something and would catch a cab later. My father, a hopeless romantic despite his extra-marital activities, saw it as an opportunity for Charlie and me to rekindle our relationship."

"Only Parker and Natalie weren't both along shortly. Natalie had originally planned to get Parker into the garage somehow so that the two of you could proceed with your plan. Instead, she was stuck in a cab halfway across town."

Morgan nodded, pacing the length of the sterile concrete floor, her boots echoing with each step. "After I got the text from Natalie, I had to improvise and intercept Parker before he made it to his car. So I jogged—in six inch heels, I might add—the four blocks to where he'd parked. Of course, he always had it way out in Timbuktu so it didn't get dings, and given that he and Charlie were at odds, I doubted he would have asked to park in the garage."

"Wait, how did you know where he parked?" I hated to inter-ject but I was truly curious.

Morgan didn't seem to mind. "Pure luck. Father and I passed Parker getting out of his car on the way to the party. He was going into a nearby sports bar." She glanced at Natalie, who bristled at the knowledge her boyfriend stopped off for a pint while she waited for him to escort her to the party. "I just figured he had hoofed it rather than risk moving his car and losing what he considered to be a prime parking spot."

Parker had been funny that way, though I wouldn't have been surprised if he had taken a cab from the sports bar to Char-lie's building, rather than walking the four blocks. She was lucky he hadn't done that after the party, given all the alcohol he'd imbibed. I wondered how she'd known that hadn't been the case.

As if reading my thoughts, Morgan added. "Parker told Natalie he needed some fresh air and was going to walk, which she relayed to me in the text. She was also able to verify his car was still parked where I'd last seen it because her taxi drove right past it."

"You're right, you certainly got lucky. So you caught up with Parker, how did you manage to get him back to the parking garage?"

Morgan rolled her eyes as she waved a hand over her curvy physique. If Natalie was peeved by Morgan's advances on her boyfriend, she made no show of it.

"Err…ok. So you…encouraged Parker to return to the parking garage with you, then what?"

Morgan laughed. "Parker was pretty wasted, so he was fairly…compliant. Once I got him in the garage, I just popped him with a little hypodermic filled with happy juice." At my raised eyebrow, she added, "A muscle relaxant with a bit of kick. Parker was on his lips in no time." Her laugh was harsh as she recalled the memory. "Meanwhile, there was no sense alerting the first cab driver by having him turn around, so once Natalie got home, she caught another cab from a different company back to parking garage and let herself in using Charlie's key code."

"And concocted the witness to account for the entry on the time log, thereby effectively putting Charlie at the garage at the time of the murder," I added.

The way his brows were drawn, Arch may have been lost but both Morgan and Natalie managed to look impressed. "How'd you figure that out?"

"It was the dog." I shrugged. "The officer at the scene remembers your witness, Margaret O'Connor, called her dog—a small black one with pointy ears that looked like it should be wearing a plaid sweater, as he described it—Ginsburg." Morgan frowned as I clarified for the others, "Morgan and her family have a habit of naming their Scottish Terriers after Supreme Court Justices. In this case, she threw the witness' last name into the mix." The last bit did nothing to improve Morgan's surly mood, given I now had a gun barrel pressed firmly against my right temple. "If I figured that out, so will the police."

Morgan snorted. "If by police, you mean Vargas, I doubt it. His thought processes are seriously impeded by his propensity for that blond tart you call a friend."

Arch shot his cousin a bemused look. "Sounds like someone is jealous, I didn't think the cop was your type."

"Shut up, lap dog. Don't forget you're still here at my convenience. You're lucky I didn't kill you when we were kids, which, by the way, was completely out of respect to your mother."

Morgan knew how hit below the belt, that was for sure. Arch glared, crossing his arms defiantly, but said nothing. Natalie, on the other hand, chuckled under breath and for a moment, I though Morgan might cut her down, too.

I cleared my throat. "I would have thought your inside source would have told you. Vargas already knows the witness was bogus. How long do you think it's going to take him to find a correlation between a haughty lawyer friend of Charlie's—one whose father happens to be former state senator—and a witness who fits the same general description and has a similar looking dog with the same name?"

"Real smooth, Morgan," Natalie smirked. "Perhaps you should have let the ding dong socialite manage the little details after all." As Morgan's lip curled into a nasty snarl, I realized it was not all giggles and matching friendship bracelets in the world of Morgan and Natalie. And given the smug look Natalie was tossing at Morgan, it had never been.

I stepped in before the hair-pulling could ensue, "Getting back to the parking garage. Natalie returns, then what?"

Morgan continued, "We fired up Big Bess using the keys Arch had supplied and after propping Parker up, we took turns backing into him." I blanched, as did Arch.

Morgan only shrugged. "Natalie wanted to run over him but logistically, puncturing him with the tailfins was much more... efficient." Double eww.

Natalie nodded in agreement. "Either way, it was messy. But at least..." she smiled, not in a pretty way, "we finally got to stick it to Parker." Morgan's boisterous laughter filled the room, as Natalie joined in. I shook my head, disgusted by what these two considered common ground.

"Ok. That's...interesting. How did you keep from damaging Charlie's car?"

Natalie clapped her hands. "Morgan found some mattresses in the garage's storage room still covered in heavy duty plastic. We placed them behind Parker to cushion the blows between the car and the block wall. It worked out great." Morgan nodded, clearly pleased with her creative use of bedding.

Arch wasn't as thrilled by this news, "Wait a minute, you used those mattresses from the storage room? I've been sleeping on Parker's...innards?" That would certainly teach him to ask before taking items that weren't his the next time around. I doubted he was thinking along those lines as his expression changed from exasperation to repulsion. I couldn't disagree as I fought to keep my own gag refluxes from engaging. Morgan and Natalie appeared bored and maybe even a bit annoyed by Arch's outburst.

After confirming Arch wouldn't projectile vomit on anyone, Morgan moved on, "Anyway, we'd had our fun with Parker, but were on a timetable and still had to clean up and deposit him else-where before the sun made its way over the horizon. We were just about finished—Parker was wrapped, Big Bess was wiped down, the mattresses stripped of their plastic and placed back into the storage room—when Charlie entered the garage."

Natalie giggled. "OMG, I was so freaked! Remember how we'd just finished pulling Parker out into the middle of the garage so we could transfer him to my car? I was so sure he'd see us."

Morgan nodded. "I know, we barely pulled Parker back into the shadows in time. Charlie was still drunk from the party, otherwise who knows what would have happened. We certainly hadn't expected him to go out for a walk at that hour." I wondered if the two of them had been stalking Charlie, but decided the real question was how long they'd been doing it.

"But, as it turned out, Charlie ended up leaving us with some parting gifts. His muddy shoes were enough of a treat, but when he accidentally dropped his tie? It was just icing on the cake. Of course, his access code was logged when he entered the garage, but the police erroneously assumed he'd returned to clean up after dumping Parker in the lake. We couldn't have planned it any better." Despite the near-misses, Morgan seemed smug while Natalie continued to giggle. I silently wished she had an off button.

"So, Charlie leaves. You collect his shoes and tie and Parker…and…" I gestured for them to continue.

Morgan scoffed. "Easy, Slick—we'd like the opportunity to revel in the moment."

Unless my ears were deceiving me, I was pretty sure I heard Arch mutter "psychos" under his breath. I might have agreed with him on that point, but wasn't about to form an alliance with him. I'd seen enough horror movies to know what happened to the third wheel. Before the end of the first act, they always ended up dead meat.

* * *

After the two took their requisite revelation time, whatever that entailed, Morgan proceeded, "Natalie ran back and grabbed her car, which we had prepped in advance to transport Parker. Once we had him tucked safely inside, I placed the earring Leah dropped during the party near Big Bess. From there, we drove along Tempe Town Lake until we found a pullout with a boat launch that wasn't occupied. It didn't take us long, considering the lake hours were enforced, so we were able to pull right up and dump him out."

"Is that when you disposed of Charlie's shoes and tie?" I asked.

Natalie chuckled. "We considered it, but were afraid riffraff would find them before the police did, so I waited until later." Of course, the search party—it had been Natalie's idea. She'd not only needed a way to distribute the evidence, but control when the items were found. The large bag had seemed out of place at the time, but now made sense. She had chosen it for its functionality.

Something else had been weighing on my mind. "Was Parker even dead when you dumped him in the water?" Ramirez had already confirmed the answer but I needed to know if *they* had known.

It didn't surprise me that it was Morgan who answered, "Does it matter?"

"It does to me."

She let out a deep breath and gave me a long, hard look. "You're going to have to learn to live with disappointment then, because I don't know. I was caught up in an adrenaline rush at the time. It never occurred to me to check."

Natalie nodded before focusing on her shoes. Neither one of them had expected the question. And now they were faced with the reality of their actions.

Morgan was thoughtful, before adding, "I can tell you he was unconscious the entire time, if that soothes your mind."

"It's not my mind that needs soothing."

"Then your soul should rest easy, because Parker's went dark the minute he killed my brother," Natalie jutted out her chin defiantly, the fact she wouldn't meet my eyes told me she was anything but.

"And my mom," Arch whispered.

I had almost forgotten he was still with us. Perhaps it was what Charlie liked about him, he was present without being seen or heard. Regardless of how limited the role he had played in Morgan and Natalie's twisted little drama, it still made him deadly in my book.

CHAPTER TWENTY

Despite the tension that filled the room, I felt my own emotion bubbling to the surface—anger. Oh yeah, I was mad. Don't get me wrong. I had no allusions why Morgan and Natalie had been so forthcoming with the details of Parker's murder. They intended to kill me and likely Arch as well. Since I had nothing to lose, I asked the question I had come for, one they had not yet answered. At least, not to my satisfaction. In the end, it was the only answer that mattered.

"Why?"

Morgan looked at me, flat, soulless eyes boring into mine, lips pulled into a tight unforgiving line. While she wasn't completely devoid of emotion, what consumed her far more disconcerting. Bitterness. After everything she'd done, she'd found no comfort. No solace.

It was Natalie who replied, "Why? Haven't we thoroughly—and I might add, graciously—explained that to you?" Apparently, her emotions hadn't quite evolved the way Morgan's had.

"No, you told me who, what, when, where and how, but you conveniently left out the answer to the most important question. In the beginning, Morgan said it wasn't for revenge. Or even retribution. However, based upon all of this," I motioned to the gun Morgan was still gripping though thankfully, was no longer pointed at my head, "it appears not to be far from the truth. Parker is dead, Charlie's life is over. One draws the obvious conclusion."

"Both made choices," Natalie gritted out, "choices, with consequences."

"So you keep saying." I shrugged.

"Surely you can understand? They acted with blatant disregard. People not only suffered, they died. What about Parker's and Charlie's consequences? Why did they get to go on living their lives? Don't you get it, AJ? Don't you understand?" She was almost pleading with me.

"I do," I replied, choosing my words carefully, "but there had to have been other, less drastic means?"

"Don't you think that I…that we tried? Do you think we would have started with the most extreme measures if we hadn't already exhausted all the others? What do you take us for—monsters?" I bit my lip and drew blood to prevent myself from blurting out a response.

"We approached Parker directly—Charlie too—to no avail. Then, we spent years…*years*…attempting to engage with law enforcement, lawyers, politicians, even the Federal Trade Commission. We researched, communicated, lobbied…anything and everything we could think of to intercept Parker and no one could help us.

"The worst thing about it, we weren't even close to shutting him down. Investing may have been second nature to Parker, but he was a genius when it came to the law—almost as good as Morgan." If the comparison to Parker agitated her, Morgan made no indication, other than to resume the tapping of the gun. "When it came to the law, he was always careful to color within the lines, even if that meant coloring on it, which is where he did his best work. So while we had a lot of sympathizers, the issues were moral in nature and therefore, outside the confines of the law."

"Then if murder was the solution, why not kill them both—you said they were both culpable, after all—why not rid the world of the entire albatross?"

Natalie considered my question for a moment. "Believe me, we talked about it, even gave it some serious consideration." She chuckled. "Charlie may have the Tin Man's version of a heart but at least he has one, which means he's capable of feeling emotion. That being said, we decided the best way to deal with him was to make him feel it, through fear, humiliation, loss. That's basically the only reason he's sitting in a jail cell right now, and not in the ground eating worm dirt with Parker."

I grimaced. "Charlie could still get the death penalty."

Natalie nodded, but it was Morgan who replied, "Even if it does come to that, he'll be incarcerated for years—someone as astute as Charlie could facilitate endless appeals—meaning he'll have plenty of time to reflect on the choices he made. And the ones he should have made."

Perhaps it was just me, but their logic seemed faulty. They had killed Parker because he was too evil and incarcerated Charlie because he had condoned it. Parker may be dead in the ground, but something couldn't help but make me wonder if Charlie hadn't been the one to get the raw end of the deal.

* * *

Something else bothered me.

"Why now? Why choose Charlie's White Party to eliminate Parker?"

Natalie threw her hands up. "Parker was back at it—messing with things that weren't his, refusing to listen to anyone's rationale. We could see where it was going to go."

"It was the reason Charlie and Parker were at odds near the end," I added.

Morgan nodded. "With the new federal regulations in place, things were tougher for Parker this time around. He needed Charlie's assistance and his high-powered contacts more than he ever had in the past. To his surprise, Charlie refused."

"Ok, but it seems like Parker would have been mad at Charlie, yet at the party, the animosity went the other direction." I thought about the looks that had passed between them and couldn't recall Charlie ever looking that enraged.

Natalie's laugh came out harsh. "Oh, Parker was plenty mad, but he was convinced Charlie would change his mind."

Morgan nodded. "In the interim, he identified another solution to his problem, one that ultimately undermined Charlie, and ended their friendship."

"So Charlie caught wind of this workaround?"

"Yup, that pretty much sums it up. It was just a matter of time —Parker had already gotten his mitts on what he needed—there would have been no stopping him."

Had I not been so distracted by the gun, which had begun dancing even more briskly against Morgan's thigh, I would have sensed the swift movement behind me.

"Get up," Natalie growled, her breath hot on my ear as she pressed something cool against the base of my neck.

Morgan's laugh was harsh as I gasped in surprise. She turned and rolled the atrium windows up, allowing a gust of warm air to flood the space. The nasty look she cast over her shoulder indicated she wasn't merely interested in taking in the nightly breeze. She nodded sharply at Natalie, who initiated an attempt to shove me toward the open window with her knees, but given the difference in our heights, ended up hitting me calf-level. I seized the opportunity to head butt her, effectively knocking her off balance, but failing to dislodge the weapon from her hand. Instead, the sudden movement caused her to fire what I had previously thought to be a gun. I flinched as it discharged, belatedly realizing I was no longer in its path, though found myself up close and personal with a fully-charged stun gun as Natalie liberated it into Arch's chest.

I momentarily found myself watching in fascinated silence as Arch screeched, "What the—" before dropping to floor, the charge rendering him unconscious.

Natalie looked at her hand in surprise, but was unable to regain her footing as I plowed into her with the best offensive tackle I could muster, which resulted in a satisfying "oomph" as she sprawled on the floor.

I managed to untangle myself from Natalie and stagger to my feet, only to have Morgan headlock me from behind. At this point I had no idea where the gun was, but rage and adrenaline surged as we struggled. Morgan and I were more evenly matched in height, though I was betting I had a few extra pounds on her that I planned to use to my advantage. There was no way I was going out that window.

Not alone, anyway.

I tried to remember the moves Ramirez had shown me. I don't recall him mentioning any specific hair-pulling techniques, but as Morgan's locks fell forward, I yanked a sizable section.

"Extensions, Morgan? Seriously?" I huffed as we knocked knees. "And you had the gall to insult my hair?"

"I'm sure it'll look better with your head cracked open on the pavement," she panted, spittle blasting my cheek.

"Well, if I'm going, you're going," I replied, serving up a pointy elbow to her ribcage as I worked to position my legs behind hers.

Morgan grunted but choked out a harsh laugh. "Not likely, but you should take comfort knowing that I'm going to gut your mangy canine once I'm done with you."

That did it. She'd gone too far. Fury raged through me as I launched myself backward, taking her with me. As we twisted and fell, Morgan's head clipped the corner of one of Charlie's solid steel sculptures and we landed with a thud, our bodies intertwined in a contorted heap. Dazed, I felt blood pooling in my mouth and warming my face. Morgan's blood. Her weight was stifling as I attempted to wiggle free. I had finally gotten to my knees and was spitting out blood when I heard the gun cock. Given her current temperament, I doubted Natalie was above shooting me in the back.

"Let's try this again," she wheezed. "Get up." Painfully, I complied and started to face her. "No, don't turn around. Move your skinny butt over to the window."

I glanced down at a prone Morgan. She still hadn't moved since our fall and now blood oozed from her wound, saturating her hair and streaking Charlie's concrete floor with color. I paused to check her pulse but Natalie snapped at me. I gave Morgan one last look as I shuffled forward slowly. No sense making this easy on her.

Out of the corner of my eye I saw a flash of movement, followed by various squeaks and scuffling sounds. I spared a glance behind me, convinced the last thing I would see was the barrel of a gun. Instead, I was rewarded with an awkward, rare grin from Arch as he pinned a squirming, furious Natalie with his arms.

My eyes went wide, looking for the gun.

"There, AJ, it's there!" Arch yelled excitedly, bobbing his head toward a spot on the floor, a few feet to the right of where he'd intercepted her.

After gingerly picking the weapon up, I trained it on Natalie, who continued thrashing about while directing obscenities at us, our various body parts, our family members and pretty much the entire human civilization. I considered offering her my supply of

Borax but frankly, she required more than I presently had on hand.

"Keep a firm hold on her, Arch. She's a deceptively slippery one."

"That she is, AJ. That she is."

Despite the gravity situation, when Natalie let out a small frustrated wail, it was all I could do not to laugh.

* * *

I called Ramirez with my free hand, briefly filled him in on the situation and asked him to have Vargas send in the cavalry. After a few choice expletives from his end, I asked him to call Leah as well. Exasperated, he hung up.

A short time later, several intense-looking police officers dressed in full combat gear engulfed the penthouse, led by one very large, extremely grumpy Detective Vargas.

I surrendered the weapon to the first officer who approached me. His was bigger, after all. Once the team secured the surroundings, Vargas called in the paramedics. I waved them off, quickly pointing at Morgan, who had only just begun to regain consciousness. I hadn't wanted to meet my fate with her on the pavement down below, but I didn't want her to die here, either. After a couple of medics gave Natalie and Arch the thumbs-up, they were handcuffed without incident.

"Time for us to have a little chat, AJ," Vargas' tone was steely, but as I glanced up at him, I noticed something else lingering in his expression—he was impressed.

I nodded, carefully easing myself into the nearest chair. For once, I didn't mind its lack of comfort. I gave him my account of the events that had transpired, while another officer took notes and asked occasional questions. Once satisfied they had what they needed, Vargas dismissed the officer. We sat side by side, quietly watching as his team worked around us, in the devastation that had once been Charlie's home.

"Will this be enough to help him?" I asked after a long moment.

"It may take a few days and a mountain of paperwork, thanks to you," he teased, "but I think charges will be dropped and he'll be released."

I nodded. "I'd like to see him. We have some...unfinished business."

"For you, AJ, that can be arranged." He chuckled, just as another officer ushered a solemn, handcuffed Arch past us.

"You're a better friend than he gives you credit for," Arch commented quietly.

I knew he meant Charlie, but was I? I thought about the times I'd openly questioned his innocence. I continued to watch as Vargas skillfully directed his team and the paramedics loaded a semi-conscious Morgan onto a stretcher. I smiled a bit as I thought about her reaction when she finally woke up, wearing a pretty little peek-a-boo hospital gown while handcuffed to the bed. Suddenly, I realized I wasn't alone.

"Ajax, you get yourself into the most...interesting predicaments."

Ramirez.

* * *

"Promise me you'll never leave your house again without back-up." Before I had a chance to protest, he smirked and pretended to contemplate something. "Never mind that, I've seen your backup. Next time, please call your boyfriend—"

"Oh my gosh, Leah. Is she totally freaking out? Is Nicoh ok? *Wait*...did he say 'boyfriend'?" Belatedly, I realized that last bit had inadvertently slipped out. Too bad there wasn't a good soap for that.

Ramirez only chuckled. "Calm down, she's fine, but a little miffed you left her out of your fun. And, just so that you know, you did butt-dial her a few times."

"I did what?" I felt around for my phone, realizing it had been in my back pocket when I had pulled it out to call Ramirez.

"There was so much commotion, she thought you and I were…rolling around…until she heard Morgan saying some nasty things about Nicoh, which is when she called Vargas. He was already en route when I called him."

I couldn't decide whether to blush or cheer, so I just nodded and pursed my lips. Rolling around? With Ramirez? I must have been making quite a face because I suddenly noticed Ramirez scrutinizing me.

"Err…Morgan did make some pretty awful threats against Nicoh and both she and Natalie had some nasty things to say about Leah, too."

My feeble attempt to cover was not lost on him, though he simply nodded. "Why don't we go and see them both."

As we made our way to the elevator, I whispered, "Do you think we can keep the whole butt-dialing incident to ourselves?"

CHAPTER TWENTY-ONE

It had been a moot point. Several officers chuckled—I swore a few others glanced at my behind—when we exited the building. I started to comment but was distracted by the high-pitched squeals coming from the direction of the crowd that had formed just beyond the building's perimeter. It could have come from only one source—Leah.

After breaking free from a portly officer who attempted to keep her at bay, I was mobbed by a force so strong, I needed Ramirez to keep me upright. Nicoh stood on his haunches, his front paws braced on my shoulders as he licked me chin to crown. Contrary to the comments Natalie had made, his breath was decent. Either that or I smelled pretty bad myself. I crossed my fingers, hoping for the prior, given the proximity I had just shared with Ramirez. Once Nicoh was satisfied I had been properly greeted, he lowered himself to the ground and chastised me with a low grumble. Leah stood cautiously to one side, watching us. One look at her tear-filled eyes and I tugged her into a fierce embrace.

"We've gotta stop doing this." She sniffled. "Between people trying to kill us at high altitudes, the daily dog cleansings and the sappy hugging and crying thing, we're never going to get any decent dates."

"Tell me about it."

* * *

"Thanks for filling her up with gas." I nodded at the Mini when we reached our respective vehicles.

"It was the least I could do, especially considering you left me behind," she replied dryly.

"Hey, I left a note," I pleaded, though she waved me off, meaning I would owe her margaritas and details later.

"When they were hauling Natalie out—nice handcuffs, by the way—she saw me in the crowd and yelled that she wanted to revise her quote."

"Her quote?" Ah, the *Real Housewives* taglines we had crafted a few nights earlier over girl talk. "Do I want to hear it?" Leah shrugged, so I gestured for her to continue.

"She said 'Life is about living with no regrets. I'd rather die doing the wrong thing for the right reasons than live wishing I'd had the courage to do them at all.'"

* * *

I emerged from my house a few days later only a bit more rested and a whole lot more bruised from my tumbles with Morgan and Natalie than I remembered being when I had gone in. I promised Leah and Ramirez I'd take it easy but things hadn't turned out quite that way. Nicoh had become increasingly restless without his gal pal and after repeated attempts to get Randy Newman on his cell phone, Leah had driven to his house, only to find it locked up tight and his car gone from the driveway. After chatting with a few of the neighbors, she returned to deliver the news. Randy and

Pandora had packed up and left for Dallas a few days early. I caught up with him a day or so after that, or I should say, he left a message on my home phone. He apologized, indicating he just wasn't one for tearful goodbyes.

Meanwhile, Nicoh was sullen and lacked his usual energy. I'm certainly no expert, but our animal friends seem to feel loss, too, perhaps even more so. It was heartbreaking to watch and though Leah and I tried our best to comfort him, he refused to eat, play with his toys or even sleep on my bed, much less his own. Instead he stayed by the front door, day after day, waiting for Pandora to return. Late at night, he would howl the same sorrowful, pained song.

When I finally chose to leave the house, I did so hesitantly. Nicoh usually accompanied me but showed no interest today. He sat at his post by the door and though his eyes remained closed, I knew he was not resting. As I left, I did not promise him I would return. If I had learned anything over the past several months, no matter how well-meaning our intentions might be, no one can guarantee that. Instead I patted him on the head, told him I loved him and as I pulled the front door shut, I knew at the very least, that much was true.

CHAPTER TWENTY-TWO

Charlie was waiting for me when I arrived at my favorite Starbucks, sipping a mug of cappuccino on the patio. We hugged awkwardly before I sat down across from him with my own iced caramel sauce latte. If he was surprised by the thick layers of caramel sauce that outweighed the balance of milk and coffee, he made no comment. He'd gained some of his color back, along with a few of the pounds he'd lost. He smiled at me, almost shyly, but the warmth didn't reach his eyes, their usual spark missing, replaced by a haunted sadness.

He squinted as though trying to place something. "You didn't bring Nicoh."

I shook my head. "He still not...doing well...with Pandora being gone."

"I'm sorry."

"Me too."

He reached across the table, just enough to encourage me to raise my eyes to meet his. "I'm sorry about more than just Nicoh, you know."

"I know you are, Charlie, but—"

"AJ, please let me finish. For once, the last word is going to be mine." I chuckled—where had I heard that before? I feigned shock, making him laugh. It sounded…and looked good on him. And so, we talked, or perhaps I should say Charlie talked and I listened, mostly. Either way, it was the longest conversation the two of us had in the twenty-plus years we had known one another. And it was a doozy. We talked about growing up as kids, going off to college, falling in love, falling out of love.

Turns out, he did care for Morgan. I couldn't bear to tell him the feeling had likely never been mutual, but I think somewhere deep inside, he'd already known. We talked about the crazy, fun times he spent with Greg and the sad ones, too. He confessed he'd kept Big Bess as a reminder, so he'd never forget the feeling of hopelessness and loss Greg's death had brought him. I'll admit I had completely misjudged him on that one. And finally, we talked about Parker—the good, the bad and the demons that had consumed him until the day he died.

And just when I thought Charlie had finished surprising me, he told me about the missing hours on the afternoon of the White Party, the ones he'd previously refused to discuss. I wasn't sure whether I should hug him or punch him when he revealed he'd been working with a private detective for several months, during which time the two of them had accumulated enough proof to put a stop to Parker's shenanigans. They planned on approaching the Attorney General the day after the party and met one final time that afternoon to ensure all their ducks were in a row. The next day came, however, and Parker went missing.

"Why didn't you present your evidence once they arrested you?"

He shook his head. "Parker was dead. Nothing good would have come from causing the few loved ones he had any more suffering. No, I had to find another way to show the police I wasn't guilty of his murder."

"Which is why you declined counsel?"

He nodded. "I couldn't risk them inadvertently finding out about my investigation."

I shook my head to show my understanding, but truthfully, had to wonder about Charlie's intentions. Just how selfless had his investigation been? Had he been trying to do the right thing by having Parker investigated? Or saving himself from an equal fate by shifting the focus off his own wrong-doings and onto those of his supposed best friend and business associate? One thing was for sure, being the one to present the evidence certainly had its benefits.

It also made me wonder—if Natalie and Morgan had known about Charlie's evidence, would it have spared Parker's life? Somehow, I doubted it. It was hard to ignore the irony, though. Had Charlie moved forward—even one day sooner—Parker would have likely spent the better part of his life in prison. Instead, he would forever be buried in a lonely grave. By altering his destiny, Morgan and Natalie also changed their own, and would now take his place, as they spent their days locked away.

If Charlie had known the outcome, would he have done things differently? With Charlie you just never knew. I shook my head— when had I gotten so cynical? I was about to give the notion a kick in the pants when Charlie snapped me out of my reverie.

"See you first thing tomorrow morning then, to photograph the progress being made on the penthouse remodel? Oh, before I forget, I'd prefer if you leave the dog at home—no sense getting sued when he gets under some construction worker's foot or his tail—"

Like I said, with Charlie you never knew. For the time being, I carefully tucked the cynic back in my pocket.

* * *

Things were only a bit less convoluted when it came to the others.

Arch pled to a lesser crime as part of a plea deal with the County Attorney and even so, would spend many years inside a prison cell. There was speculation Morgan and Natalie would receive the death penalty due to the heinous nature of the crime, as well as for the lack of remorse they'd shown to date.

In a very political move, Morgan's father distanced the Conrad family from the situation. It was rumored that given her fragile state, Cecilia Conrad had not been told of her daughter's complicity in the murder of Parker Harris. Instead she was led to believe Morgan was working abroad on behalf of her law firm to facilitate relations with various foreign entities. Natalie's family attended her initial arraignment, but as details of the crime continued to emerge, they were seen less and less at court proceedings and eventually disappeared altogether from the public eye.

No one acknowledged Charlie—unless you counted Leah and me—it was as though he never existed. Surprisingly, Charlie took it as a sign to close one chapter in his life and begin a new one. How that would work out for him was anyone's guess, only time would tell. At least he'd made the effort once the opportunity presented itself, which is more than I can say for most. Morgan and Natalie had wanted to punish him, leaving him humiliated, hopeless and alone. In the end, they had lost that bet on all counts, because for all their grand plans and schemes, there was one thing they hadn't counted on.

Me.

It was a perfect day for a picnic. One of those lazy southwestern days where the sun warms your shoulders as the gentle breeze lulls you to sleep. Ramirez had selected a remote location where the only sound was from a nearby fountain that burbled as plumes of water danced to a synchronized, yet silent symphony. At least that was the way I imagined it.

A blanket had been carefully smoothed across an even patch of ground. On top he had meticulously arranged a simple but mouth-watering picnic. Even Nicoh had recently come out of hiding to join us and was happily gnawing on a gargantuan-sized dog bone—peanut butter-flavored, of course.

Ramirez laughed, tugging on a long strand of my hair as I moaned over the first bite of the peanut butter and pickle sandwich he had made, just for me. It was only after I'd polished off one half and was well into the second I realized he'd been watching me.

"What?" I mumbled, my mouth still partially-full as I batted self-consciously at the tip of my nose. "Please do not tell me I've had peanut butter on my face this entire time?" When he chuckled and shook his head, I added, "Ok, you're totally amazed by my freakish, yet amazing peanut butter and pickle sandwich-eating abilities?"

Once again, he shook his head before taking a long sip of his iced tea. "Just trying to decide something."

Intrigued, I gently placed the sandwich on its wax paper wrapper. "Um…you and Vargas and your other poker buddies aren't going to start placing bets on how many of these babies I can put away, are you? Because I'll have you know, I have a very important professional reputation to uphold."

His voice was quiet when he replied, his eyes searching mine, "I was just wondering if you thought you could ever like me as much as you do those peanut butter and pickle sandwiches." A smile tugged the corner of his mouth, but there was a hint of seriousness in his eyes…and a question.

"Well…" I could feel the heat rising in my cheeks, "these are pretty good sandwiches."

"Uh huh."

"And you did make them."

"I did."

"I suppose…in time…I could like you both equally."

"Equally, as in fifty-fifty?"

"I might be able to manage that."

"Oh?"

"Just one thing though."

"What's that?"

"Don't think for a minute you can ply me with sandwiches to improve your odds."

"I wouldn't dream of it." He leaned closer, smiling.

I put a hand firmly on his chest. "I wasn't done yet."

"Oh? Sorry. What else?"

"Don't ever think about sharing your second peanut butter and pickle sandwich with anyone else."

"It's a deal." Our lips met just as his phone buzzed, causing us both to shift back in surprise.

"Better get that." I started to reach for the rest of my sandwich.

Ramirez smiled. "Still aren't sure about that fifty-fifty, are you?" Before I could answer, he stood and moved a short distance away to take the call.

"What are you looking at?" I grumbled at Nicoh, whose tongue flopped lazily as he zeroed in on my sandwich. Having missed his opportunity, he emitted his own rumble before crossing his paws, continuing the destruction of the monster bone.

Ramirez returned moments later, his happy mood gone.

"What?" I struggled to get out. "What is it?"

"That was my contact with the FBI."

"Ok…"

"Winslow Clark escaped from the federal prison where he was being held. They think he broke out three weeks ago."

"*Think?* Oh…no…no…" At least now I knew the identity of my mystery texter and caller, for whatever that was worth.

"It's worse, AJ."

"Just tell me, Ramirez. Please tell me. Is he…is he coming to get me?"

He shook his head, looking me straight in the eye. "He's already here."

I groaned.

Couldn't a peanut butter and pickle sandwich ever just be a peanut butter and pickle sandwich? I thought to myself as Nicoh engulfed the rest in one noisy bite.

Nope. Life is never that simple.

~ The End ~

ABOUT HARLEY

Harley Christensen lives in Phoenix, Arizona with her significant other and their mischievous motley crew of rescue dogs (aka the "kids").

When not at her laptop, Christensen is an avid hockey fan and lover of all things margarita. It's also rumored she's never met a green chile or jalapeño she didn't like, regardless of whether it liked her back.

For more information on the author and her books, please visit her at www.mischievousmalamute.com.

OTHER BOOKS BY HARLEY

Mischievous Malamute Mystery Series
Book 1 ~ Gemini Rising
Book 2 ~ Beyond Revenge
Book 3 ~ Blood of Gemini
Book 4 ~ Deadly Current
Book 5 ~ Gemini Lost
Book 6 ~ Fatal Bonds
Book 7 ~ COMING SOON!

Six Seasons Suspense Series
Book 1 ~ First Fall
Book 2 ~ Winter Storm